the

VASTER

WILDS

the

VASTER
WILDS

Lauren Groff

RIVERHEAD BOOKS

NEW YORK ◆ 2023

RIVERHEAD BOOKS
An imprint of Penguin Random House LLC
penguinrandomhouse.com

Library of Congress Cataloging-in-Publication Data

Names: Groff, Lauren, author.
Title: The vaster wilds / Lauren Groff.
Description: New York : Riverhead Books, 2023.
Identifiers: LCCN 2022039817 (print) | LCCN 2022039818 (ebook) |
ISBN 9780593418390 (hardcover) | ISBN 9780593418413 (ebook)
Subjects: LCGFT: Novels.
Classification: LCC PS3607.R6344 V37 2023 (print) | LCC PS3607.R6344 (ebook) |
DDC 813/.6—dc23/eng/20220831
LC record available at https://lccn.loc.gov/2022039817
LC ebook record available at https://lccn.loc.gov/2022039818

International edition ISBN: 9780593715864

Printed in the United States of America
1st Printing

BOOK DESIGN BY LUCIA BERNARD

For my sister, Sarah

the

VASTER
WILDS

I.

The moon hid itself behind the clouds. The wind spat an icy snow at angles.

In the tall black wall of the palisade, through a slit too seeming thin for human passage, the girl climbed into the great and terrible wilderness.

Over her face she wore a hood drawn low, and she was slight, both bony and childish small, but the famine had stripped her down yet starker, to root and string and fiber and sinew. Even so starved, and blinded by the dark, she was quick. She scrabbled upright, stumbled with her first step, nearly fell, but caught herself and began to run, going fast over the frozen ruts of the field and all the stalks of dead corn that had come up in the summer already sooty and fruitless and stunted with blight.

Swifter, girl, she told herself, and in their fear and anguish, her legs moved yet faster.

———

These good boots the girl had stolen off the son of a gentleman, a stripling half her age but of equal size, who had died of the smallpox the night before, the rash a rust spreading over the starved bones. These leather gloves and the thick cloak the girl had stolen off her own mistress. She banished the thought of the woman still weeping upon her knees on the frozen ground in the courtyard inside that hellish place. With each step she drew away, everything there loosened its grip on the girl.

Yet there was a strange gleam upon the dark ground of the field ahead, and as she moved, she saw it was the undershirt of the soldier who a fortnight earlier had been caught worming his body slow from the horrors of the fort and toward the different horrors of the forest. He had made it halfway to the trees when in silence a shadow that had lain upon the ground grew denser, grew upward, came clear at last as the fearsomest of the men of this country, the warrior two heads taller than the men of the fort, who made himself yet more terrible by wearing upon his shoulders outstretched a broad dark mantle of turkey feathers. He had lifted with one hand the creeping fearful soldier by his hair and had with a knife cut a long wet red mouth into the man's throat. Then he dropped him to spill his heart's blood into the frozen earth and there the dead man lay splayed ignoble. All this time, he had lain unburied, for the soldiers of the settlement had become too weak and too cowardly in their hunger to fetch the body back.

She had passed the dead man and his reek had drawn itself out of her nostrils and she was nearly to the woods when she stumbled again, for the thought of these two men gave rise to thoughts of other men who lurked perhaps in the woods, men out there hidden and awaiting her. And now, as she peered before her into the dark of the forest, she saw a man crouching in ambush in ever deeper blacker shadow of each tree, perhaps a man with a knife or an ax or an arrow and cold murder in his eye.

She stopped her running for a breath, but she had no choice, she took her courage up again and she ran on.

And as she ran each imagined man in passing revealed himself to be mere shadow again.

She had chosen to flee, and in so choosing, she had left behind her everything she had, her roof, her home, her country, her language, the only family she had ever known, the child Bess, who had been born into her care when she was herself a small child of four years or so, her innocence, her understanding of who she was, her dreams of who she might one day be if only she could survive this starving time.

Think not of it, girl, she told herself, think not of it, else you shall die of grief.

And she did not turn back to look upon the gleam of the fort's fires as they painted the night sky above in red. She was unlettered but was deep devout, a good and a pious girl, and she had listened when the ministers read from the holy book, she had tracked their words and taken them whole in long phrases into her knowledge. She had learned the lesson of only forward movement from the wife of Lot, who had glanced backward once as she was fleeing the destruction of sodom and by her weakness and the wrath of god had been transformed to a pillar of salt.

Only when she was inside the forest did the wind remove its hands from her cheeks and from under her skirts. It was warmer among the trees but by no means warm. She stopped and pressed her forehead to the rough bark of a pine and the harshness of it on her skin held her there. What light that could have fallen from the sky did not fall at all, as the heavens above were covered by a thickness of cloud. The forest before her was as dense as pitch, though pocks of snow did gleam in the pits of the trees. Her breath was ragged and with effort she quieted it. She let the silence seep back into her, into the forest, and it smoothed over the memory of her crashing footsteps, and she wondered if she had been loud enough to have waked the men of the fort or the original men of this forest. The men known, the men unknown. Either could be creeping near to her even now.

She listened over the scrape and bow of the wind, cold trunk rubbing trunk in a tuning of fiddles, but she heard no footsteps and no breaking twigs. Though the lack of sound was no real solace.

At last, when her blood calmed in her ears, she heard the stream not far from her, the water rasping under its shell of ice. She pressed forward as fleet and soft as she could, and when under her foot she discovered the slickness of the ice, then the narrow aisle of stony bank where the stream ran swollen in the spring, she followed it northward, grateful to escape the sharp grasping twigs and bushes that snatched at her face and her clothing.

————

Into the night the girl ran and ran, and the cold and the dark and the wilderness and her fear and the depth of her losses, all things together, dwindled the self she had once known down to nothing.

A nothing is no thing, a nothing is a thing with no past.

It was also true that with no past, the girl thought, a nothing could be free.

In time, her mind that had been shocked in flight began to move into thinking again.

She became aware of eyes upon her.

And though she imagined that they were the hostile eyes of men, they were in fact the eyes of the forest itself watching this new form of creature with its wheezing breath and crashing footfall and bitter human reek, all the night birds and the roaming creatures stilled in silent wonderment as the girl went past. And even when the creatures could no longer see or hear the running girl and the last scent of her distress faded in their immediacy from the noses of the crawling beasts, when only a trace of her could be scented upon the leaves and dirt and snow displaced by her feet, the forest's sense of time shuddered and jerked forward, and the rip that the running girl made became healed, and the ordinary business of the creatures' hungers was reawakened behind her. Only hours after she had passed through the forest, she became to them a strange dream barely remembered in the urgencies of the moment.

———————

It was perhaps minutes, perhaps hours, there was no way to tell, but a long thick expanse of time spent running northward up the stream bank, when the girl saw a deeper darker shine near where her boot fell, a softness of the ice beneath, and she knew it to be water freed from its frozen crust, openly flowing. She bent and took off her leather gloves with her teeth and pressed her unworking hands between her legs until they had thawed enough to bend, then she opened the sack that she had been carrying in one stiff fist, reached in and took the pewter cup she had stolen, dipped it into the running water, and drank deep. The cold sliced down the center of her like the tip of a knife. It made her ache. Her teeth chattered in the bones of her skull. Her stomach, which had been empty these four days, protested at its new fullness of water. She replaced the cup and tied the sack to her waist, lifting her cloak and gowns to put it against her skin so she could feel it on the flesh of her body and would be comforted by having it always near. She wanted to sink down into the small heap of snow to sleep, her head swam and pounded, but she could not do this she knew, and she pressed herself on again, forward, away, farther.

And as she ran she prayed in her soul: O god, by whom the meek are guided in judgment, and light riseth up for the godly, grant me in all my doubts and uncertainties the grace to ask what thou wouldst have me do that the spirit of wisdom may save me from all false choices and that in thy light I may see light and in thy straight path may not stumble.

She listened for anything, for the low moan of a night bird as emissary of the divine, a shifting quality of wind that would speak its will to her, but in response there were only the noises of her passage and the cold wind playing against the disinterested forest.

And thus she ran again, and while running as soft as she could, she remembered the solace of song and thought perhaps it could heat the edges of her fear until it melted within her.

So only inside herself she sang as brightly as she knew how, the spring clad all in gladness doth laugh at winter's sadness fa la la la la la la la la la la and so on.

She knew many songs, of course, but this was the only one that came forth to meet her, quite a strange absence of song there was inside her mind, as once a lifetime ago she had been a dancing quipping sing-ing little fool and hundreds of songs she had known. But she knew that a fool could only exist where there was indulgence and freedom enough for laughter and so it was natural that in flight all of her other songs had dissolved. Still, this one song gave what comfort it could, though in such exigency such comfort was small.

The moon had begun to show its face and the woods were bands of light and dark with snow passing in its streaks beneath.

Something tore in the skies above and the new downsifting snow was no longer needles of ice as it had been when she had first escaped the fort but had become now soft slow flakes that began to collect upon the old surface of snow and to obscure the steps she had made behind her.

Thank you good snow for your aid, the girl thought.

Press on, girl, the snow said, in falling.

———

It was not long afterward that the voices descended to her from the sky.

At first, she could not distinguish what they said, but soon they spoke to her louder and slid into the mistress's tones, scolding. Wicked sprite, verminous bit of stuff, thou last least unlettered Zed, who fled thy duty in thy mistress's worst need. For it is said thou must submit thyself unto the elder, yea all be subject one to another and be clothed with humility, for god resisteth the proud and giveth grace to the humble.

So the voice of the mistress hissed to her out of the dark forest.

And forgetting herself the girl said aloud into the falling snow, Ah but does the good book not say also to escape to the mountains lest ye be consumed?

And she laughed because she knew it did say this and that she had won the point.

But the forest grew wary at the laugh, this new noise made within its sleeping stillness, and the girl had to slap her own cheek to hush herself and goad her body forward.

The mistress's voice fell itself a flake and the girl in her running left it behind her.

Now the moon came full out from its cloudy coverlet and the night grew old. The girl was so weary, so weary. She was running on little anymore but the air in her lungs and the forward thrust of her terror. Her breath was visible in white plumes that floated off upward behind her.

And a new voice said in her ear, Why, girl, do you bend your feet to the north?

I run toward living, I run toward the living, the girl told this new voice. Away from a certain wretched death, away from the devil that prowls invisible in the settlement. Toward what I once peeped over the governor's shoulder, a parchment, a map, a fat bay drawn to the east and a ladder of rivers like the sun's rays that climbed ever northward out of it. He was stabbing the drawing with his fat finger, the governor, saying to the man beside him that up here at the top of the lands drawn, in the north, there were the settlements of frenchmen, canada, and in the south here there were settlements of spanishmen, la florida. And in gathering quick-quick the stuff in the sack just before my flight, I did bethink to myself that though both frenchmen and spanishmen are foul papists of course, they are still the men of a similar god, of the same holiest of books. And that because it seemed equal distance north and south to the settlements, I must choose the frenchmen, for I do not speak a whit of the spanish language, but of the french I have had a small taste and can make myself understood.

And yet you do not know the scale of this place? the voice said, and it was now scornful.

And the girl said, No, but surely it must be smaller than my own far greater country across the waters, where each field is so thick with legend and myth and ancient battles that one step is not merely in space, unlike in this new world, but also through layers of time. Here there is nothing, only land, all the earth and mountains and trees remain innocent of story. This place is itself a sheet of parchment yet to be written upon.

And what, the voice said, should you even survive the journey, would you expect such foul papists to do to a young girl like you, to a young body like your own young female person?

O do not bend my thoughts to such evil end, she said sternly.

But the voice persisted, And you who had only ever known comfort and company, who had slept all your life beside other warm bodies, you who have sought out other humans even if you were a single moment alone, for solitude was unbearable to you, are you so ready to be utterly without friend in these echoing wastes?

And she wanted to weep but she did not and instead she said, But I am not alone for I carry my god in my heart always.

And she did, she felt god, a pinprick of light deep within her.

But the voice said, And what if the lasting peril is not man at all but god's own wilderness, the dangerous landscape, the beasts that roam and prey in this place?

And now she thought for the first time of the deathly cold of these days at the end of winter, then of the wolves and the mountain lions and the serpents that made a home in this wild uncivilized land.

And these were but the known perils, but she thought there must also be perils unknown. Monsters uncharted to the imagination of man, difficulties impossible to return from.

When she was quite small and the mistress's son Kit was not bent on the torment of her, the few times he had softened somewhat and took her upon his knee and showed her the terrible things in his books, she had seen a picture of a headless man with eyes set deep within his shoulders and a mouth under his ribs. A man with the head of a dog. And Kit would also tell her astonishing things, things educated boys knew, for instance of the lemures, who were shades of the malignant dead, and the places in the ocean where sailors were on one side sucked down into a chewing maw or on the other plucked from the ship by an enormous

beast and gobbled. Riddling women with bodies of lions. The spiteful
fairies of the woods who stole children to raise them in the lands under
the hills and left squeaking babies made of clay in their place. And what
was not writ in a book or told to her by Kit, her own quick and teeming
mind could create, for instance a woman with the teeth of a viper or a
black mist of poison sleeking low in wait.

She knew that surely such monsters could thrive in a place so vast
and varied as this place was.

And of course even the most redoubtable of the men of the fort were
terrified of the worst terrors that the forest held, not the bears or monsters, but the intelligent man who hated and would slyly murder them.

Then again she had lived among the men of the fort long enough to
understand that even among her own, too, there were bad men, for there
had been gentlemen the girls all whispered to stay away from and soldiers with a red gleam of the devil to them and mercenaries who killed as
easy as sleeping, and it would be one of these who would be sent after
her, for she knew that at least one bad man would be sent after her, for
what she had done could not be permitted to stand.

She shuddered and had to put from her thought the tortures this bad
man would do unto her if indeed she were caught.

For even a good man was more deadly than the worst of bears, and
she had seen what even a blind ancient bear with its teeth pulled out of
its black gums and its claws cut off and its eyes blinded in pink cross-
hatching could do. In the gardens upon the south bank, in the summer
heat, she stood among the watching people in their finery, in their sickness of excitement; and her eyes could not be drawn away from where
in the ring the heavy stinking slavering miserable bear had been tied to

the stake. Yet when the ferocious dogs were loosed to tear at the matty miserable beast, the bear did calmly throw them, one two three, until all three dogs were broken and whimpering and the curs pulled themselves off with their front legs to discover some place to die in peace alone. And all around, the people jeered at the beasts both victorious and slain. But the girl had walked home carrying an ice of horror in her entrails, and that night the poor old bear entered into the worst of her nightmares, showing its gums with the abscesses of green pus until she sickened woke to the churchbells of morning. And this famous fighting bear was merely a city bear, unused to the thicker older forests of this new wild place, he was a bear that had been tamed. A wild bear would be many times more vicious and brutal than what she had known, like everything from this benighted land. It would be unthinkable in its scale and ferocity. And men would be worse.

Her body was staggering now, her breath rasped in the cold air.

She must have come leagues from the fort, she told herself, and she dared to look behind her now toward where the fort would have been. But she could find no traces of its light upon the sky, no sign that her people had come to this place at all. And this was good.

The voice came back once more to say calmly, Once a fool, ever a fool.

Silence, she cried out to the voice inside her mind. And the voice obeyed and made itself silent. And she was left all alone in the terrible darkness again.

2.

She kept running, though too tired, she ran until the light of the moon waned and her body in its many hours of running had settled into a hot exhilaration.

All at once, she breathed the cold with gladness, and her legs felt light and free. Her skin prickled full of fire.

And when this joy of running arose in her, there also arose small visions that passed before her eyes.

There, within the shape of an elm uprooted by some distant windstorm, its gnarled roots dark against the night, she saw rearing a stallion black and shining.

But no, girl, she told herself, there are no stallions in this new world, for the only horses to be found in this place had been brought upon the ships, and they had been eaten long ago in the deepening hungers of the famine.

Later, from the top of a rise, she saw in the dim and silvery light the wind lifting lighter snow and sculpting it into a shining city with rooftops and chimneys and a steeple and even the smoke of fires merrily ascending from the chimneys toward heaven, and it gladdened her heart so well that she cried out aloud. Then the wind shifted and dashed the fairy city into the ground.

And, in devastation, she ran on.

At last, the stream that she had been following grew wide and the trees in the dimness split open to show a space of vast cold dying moonlight ahead. And there it was, the river, iced in its greenish white, and beneath the surface lay deep and angry waters that churned ever outward, first toward the bay then out into the larger colder wilder oceans.

And this river was so far from where she had begun her flight that it was unlikely, she decided, that even so bloodthirsty a man as any who would be sent after her from the fort would make it to this place before giving up and creeping defeated home. For all the souls who had come over to this country were now at the end of this winter of horror starved, and many of the very stoutest had hungered and shat and coughed themselves into the final kingdom of death, and even the most vicious of the men who had come across the ocean had weakened and become strangely indolent, lying on their cots all day and staring blankly at the gray and ice-pissing ice-shitting skies.

At the border of the river, she discovered a crevice within the boulders that was barely larger than her own body, and she moved swiftly to make it a hovel of her own, for the first new light of the day was

now growing in the east and she would be soon plain visible to anyone about.

Down in the cleft, away from the blow of wind, she warmed her hands
again under her skirts in the hot split of her thighs. When her fingers
could move, she untied the sack and set out her few precious things: the
two brown coverlets that, though crawling with lice, were thick and
warm, then the biting hatchet, then the knife, then the pewter cup so
palely glowing, then the flint.

These were all the goods she had thought to bring with her in the
moment of rupture. She would have brought food, but there had been
no food to steal for many days.

When she had warmed herself enough in the cleft out of the hard wind,
she ran to a pine tree with dead boughs and snapped them off and
dragged them back over the rocks and stepped upon them until they
were small enough to bring down into the hole with her. She took a
handful of dry brown needles from their cling on the smallest twigs.
She crouched in the hole and struck and struck and struck at the flint
with the knife's hilt, but no spark leapt up. She struck yet more until her
hands were numb and her face was wetted with tears in her despair.

Spark, fall upon this leaf and become flame, she whispered.

Almighty father, thy servant begs for help.

But for a long while, the spark was deaf to her pleas, and she had to
warm her hands between her legs twice more to make them able to
move again.

Finally, though, a spark fell and she cradled it with dry needles and dead leaves and breathed upon it, and the spark was shy, it nearly flicked itself dead again, but she prayed and blew again, and it grew, it was hungry, it ate a small bite of the dead leaf and found that it wanted more, it licked up and became flickering joyous flame. She fed it until it became a small and hot fire that she was so grateful for and so delighted in its warmth that she had the longing to put it in her own mouth to eat it up.

The flame danced prettily, moving its pert little head all around like a living creature. When she was sure it was strong enough that it would not be extinguished, she spat into it for good luck.

Now, over the top of her hovel, she spread one of her woolen coverlets to make a flat tent, and she wrapped the other coverlet around her body, and in the new warmth of the fire, in the tent's darkness, the stones all around her took on warmth. What flakes of snow could land upon the hot stones near the fire hissed out. Her body, breath by breath, released its tautness. She felt strange and soon realized that the strangeness came from not shivering for the first time she could remember in many months. Her run over these miles in the night and this new fire had warmed her enough to calm the unwilled shuddering of her body. For, within the misery of the fort, all the firewood had run out over the long course of the siege, and what wood that could be spared of the torn-down houses was meant to warm the gentlefolk first, and she, being a mere servant, though once the pet of the liberal and artistic household, had been abandoned among the lesser folk to the sharp and gnawing teeth of the cold. She could only creep by night, made icicle in the day, to the warmth of the child Bess's fevered body to take what she could from Bess's spare flesh and try to warm her in return.

The comfort of her hovel now was so mightily unexpected that it soothed the sharpness of her panic and horror, and she fell into a quick deep sleep. She slept so full that if a beast had neared and licked her face, or if the sharp and slinking soldier who was even now following her tracks through the dawn had leapt these many miles in a blink and silently stolen upon her with a knife in his hand, she could not have waked enough to find herself afraid.

3.

On the surface of the ice, small curls of snow and wind whipped in doggish frenzy.

The light strengthened, and the far side of the river shone clear and sharp out of the dark.

Across the ice, if the girl had been awake and watching, she would have seen a trail of women and children who had been born to this land, walking in a loose line from their village to the boulders of the bank. Soon, two fires leapt up and revealed how the ice had been cut neatly from the river for the fetching of water and for bathing.

In the dawn light, the distant bodies walked into the water, and there they bathed despite the cold, running quickly in and splashing about then running just as quickly out to warm their bodies near the fires, these dozens of well-fed women and children, gleaming in the firelight and the shy dawn. Had she been near, the girl would have seen that they wore paint a half inch thick, a mix of fat and herb and clay that kept them warm in the winters and shaded in the hot months and safe from biting insects in all seasons. She would have seen that they were not naked as her own people presumed but rather clothed in a splendid lissome clothing worn close to their skin, which bent as they bent and moved as they moved.

Although she was deep within her sleep, the girl opened her eyes and sat up and looked all about, and while she was dreaming, she saw the small forms on the other side of the river cooking their meat and their bread, the mothers tossing bits of moss high in the air and each child shooting the moss with tiny arrows, even the smallest, who wobbled on their pins but still shot. Skimmed over the water came the voices indistinct and laughter so warped by distance and wind and her heavy sleep that she believed such sounds to be the sounds of the city of her birth as it awakened into day.

After the noise that came thick across the frozen water, there came the smell of their cooking and the mingled smoke, and the girl smelled it within the depths of her slumber, but as she had so vividly imagined food all throughout the long starving time in the fort, imagined it so that it was almost real, that even within her dream she believed the food to be dream food.

Still, her mouth moved in chewing and swallowing until, inside her dream, her appetite was contented.

She closed her dreaming eyes full and lay back and slept deep again, and as she slept into the morning, the people put out their fires and faded up the path back to their village.

———

She slept and she slept, and as she did, into the girl's mind came the night terrors.

These were not strangers to her, the night terrors; they had visited her since long before she had learned language, when all the world was startling and new, and when under the skin of her perception it seemed that awful things did constantly beat.

It was now that she saw beasts made of fleshless bone rise out of the meadows of this place with plaques of clay falling from their joints and shattering upon the ground, and their knobs clacked as they moved, and they were all black and sere, for in such a gray and desert meadow as the one she saw in her terror, only the dead could walk their phantom bones.

These visions had become worse in her hunger, though she had had them as bad companions in her sleep always and was used to waking in anguish for the things that she had seen.

Even back in the mistress's house in the city, fed until she could eat and drink no more and bedded down upon green reeds strewn with fresh herbs, she had seen curious horrors of sleep: vultures made of night, oily pools of darkness gathering on the ceiling above, growing the way drops of rainwater grow, descending toward her bearing fanged and screaming faces.

When she woke now, alone within her cleft, the night terrors had soured the comfort she had taken in the warmth and she felt echoing and empty inside.

All her life, she had awoken thinking first of the child Bess, of her hunger, her need, her happiness. Now that there was no child Bess to think of, she was struck to stone, for she did not know how to think first of herself.

The fire was still a few glowing ants. Her body was so wretched sore from her flight that she gasped when she bent to blow the flames alive again. The coverlet above her head was wet from what flakes the wind had tossed there, which melted in her warmth.

She sent her mind back the distance that she had walked in the night and tried to feel if she was being followed over it.

She sniffed the air as if it could tell her.

But the distance she had come and the air she smelled said nothing to her at all.

The world, the girl knew, was worse than savage, the world was unmoved.

It did not care, it could not care, what happened to her, not one bit.

She was a mote, a speck, a floating windborne fleck of dust.

As she lay in the warm stone cleft, she felt the decision she must make waiting in her. Either she would cross the perilous and melting river or she would press westward on this very bank and try to find a narrow place farther along to ford the water. Her tongue felt too large in her mouth and stiff and dry, so she took the hatchet and the cup and rose, groaning despite her need for silence, for her pain was extreme sharp.

She crept over the boulders on her hands and knees, risking being seen by any eyes that might be watching on the other bank. She made her way into the darker day of the forest.

As she crawled and crept, she felt old in her bones with her hunger and cold but kept moving toward the sound of the brook. There she crouched on the knobby knees of a wide oak and lifted her skirts, and the cold pawed at her bared buttocks as she squatted and pissed so hot that the piss returned up to her face in steam. There was an opening in the brook where the water ran freely in the ice behind a boulder, and she carefully slid out over the ice and knelt at the edge of the water and scooped and drank from her cup until her head fairly swam with cold.

She removed the gloves, and closing her eyes to not see how they were stained red, she plunged her hands into the frigid water and scrubbed and scrubbed, but when she brought them out again, no longer feeling as though they belonged to her, she saw there were still rings of blood around her nails, and she put the gloves on hurriedly to hide them and warm her hands again.

Then she looked down and saw that the crescent of her boot's heel upon the ice had revealed something gleaming. She looked closer. It was a golden eye that was staring up at her, unblinking.

Then she rubbed harder to discover that it was the head of a large fish that had been frozen within the ice there, its blue lips pressed in a kiss to the surface.

O do not cry, girl, she told herself sternly upon the astonishment of this gift, but still the world went hot and liquid in her eyes.

She had been delivered. Gracious lord, I thank thee for thy mercy, she said aloud.

And she took her hatchet up in her hand and carefully chipped away at the ice around the fish's head, then she freed its gills with careful carving, then its body at an angle to the top of the ice, its ridged topfin and the side fins and the fat pale belly beneath. She was delicate and she was slow and she tried to keep the sound of her chipping muffled with her cloak.

But by the time her knees had frozen upon the ice, she had lost her patience and hacked away to free the fish, though in her impatience she left a large remainder of its tail stuck in the ice.

And then she shoved the hatchet and cup into her bodice to hold them as she bent and took the fish up in her arms, and in her weakness and slightness, she could barely lift it, and she rose to her feet and it was so heavy and so cold that she let it fall down again upon the ice, where it thumped hard. For a moment, she considered the half fish upon the ice, then she kicked it forward so it slid toward the bay.

In this way, kicking and sliding, she pushed the frozen fish toward her little cleft in the boulders, where, she hoped, the fire was still burning and warming the stones and the air there. And as she went, the fish first left its scales in a shining silvery trail, then it began to lose its fatty skin, threads of which she picked up and put in her mouth to savor. Her stomach, so long empty, revolted at the taste.

At last, she and her fish reached the wider river, where she was painfully visible should there happen to be eyes watching her, which, she sensed, there were. She hoped the eyes were merely those of the crows thick in the border trees, which were loudly discussing her struggles with the fish and laughing down with their cracked and scornful voices.

With haste, she pushed the fish up the flakier ice at the river's edge until finally she saw the coverlet spread like moss over the top of the stone enclosure, and she put her hands in the gills on both sides of the fish's head and tugged it backward up over the rocks of the shoreline and kicked it into her little hole, where her fire had diminished again to the thinness of a candle's flame.

When she inserted her body under the tent of the coverlet, the fish was so large that it seemed there was no space remaining for her own body. She stared at the gaping fish head, then took up the knife in her hand and split the fish's skin at the belly, and with the blade she peeled it away from the frozen flesh. The meat was so iced that it resisted the knife, and she could not risk the smells and smoke of cookery. She took the surface of the pale muscle and sliced a fine sheet of flesh off it and set this sheet of flesh upon her tongue, and there to her rejoicing mouth it melted and became sweet and buttery and dissolved down her throat.

It had been four days since she had eaten, since a broth of peppery carrotlike roots that, in the height of her frenzy and desperation, she had stolen out of the fort at midnight to wrestle up from the frozen ground.

For the child Bess was dying, wasting away into nothing. Pale blue lips, cold cheeks.

The searing loneliness when the child Bess would not open her eyes.

There had been a hillside that she had seen in the fall that had been covered over in a fine white lacy flower that seemed familiar to her, that smelled when she had absently plucked one of the flowers like a vegetable in the markets at home. And when the need had become so extreme it looked as though all the settlement would perish from it, she risked a slit throat and squeezed herself out the cut in the palisade and crept into the forest, flying through the treacherous night to the hillside and finding the hillside now covered in snow and digging in plain view with the hatchet that in her later flight had become one of her only friends. Then when the hatchet could not bite hard enough into the stony ground, she scrabbled with her hands. And then, frozen to stiffness, her breath in floating white plumes in the air, she stole like a low thing back through the dawn, back through the slit.

Within the dangers of the sleeping fort, she discovered for herself a place hidden from eyes and pulled a good broad lintel from an abandoned and skeletal house and built a fire and stole a kettle, and as the dawn light strengthened and the day became plain, she peeled the roots as swiftly as her frozen-numb fingers could manage and hacked them to pieces and dropped them into the boiling water. And then, with kicks and curses and thrown stones, she kept off the children who had crept out from their beds and were watching the cooking with the starved and avid faces of street dogs.

But soon she relented, for they were children, and she threw them the peelings and they crammed them into their mouths, dirt and all.

Snow had begun to fall when the soup had finished its cooking, just at the point when it was edible, and she lifted the heavy kettle in her hands and ran in the shadows through the lanes, where any man walking abroad at that hour could easily have stopped her and stolen for himself what she was bearing home. But she met no man out walking and felt sick in her relief when she found herself within the broad hall of the governor's house, where the sick and the dying and the powerful souls of the settlement were kept.

She rushed through the rows of the vomiting and shitting and dead people, past the manic starved who shouted out when they smelled hot food passing, and came at last to her mistress and the minister and the dear child Bess who lay dying in her chilly cot.

She brushed the pale hair from the child Bess's forehead and kissed her and smelled the sweetness of her body eating itself for fuel, and she quickly poured out a bowl of the soup and blew upon the spoon to cool it and brought it with her trembling hand to the child Bess's lips, but the child's lips and teeth remained clenched against it. She let the precious soup dribble out onto her bolster. Her face had grown gaunt and sunken out of its pale round moonlike beauty, and her skin was as waxy and yellow as horn, and her fair hair had darkened with the grease and sweat of dying.

But she was dying of no disease, this sweet innocent idiot, no disease save the horror of this place. She, who had precious few thoughts rustling about her mind, was dying of a thought.

And it was the slow and intentional death of the child Bess that had driven the girl into the forest to dig up the flowers' roots, she would do anything it would take to bring the child Bess, her own dearest heart, back from the border of death.

There was a rustle, a movement, and she saw the mistress and her husband the minister sit up avid with the smell of the food, and to keep them from snatching up the hot kettle, she poured out a bowl for her, for him, and they gobbled up their own soup so quickly while it was so hot that yellow blisters rose upon their lips and tongues and gums.

When it proved that the child Bess still would not eat after the cajoling in whispers, after the girl tried wedging her teeth apart with the tip of the spoon, the minister, the mistress's second husband, reached out his hands and snatched up the child Bess's bowl.

But the girl, whose body was still frozen after her long night in the field, with her struggle with the icy earth and the terror of being discovered, saw this and hated the minister in the fullness of her heart and grabbed back the child Bess's bowl in her own hands and drank down the soup inside, staring her master in the eye.

For, though he had all the rights to what she had made of her own hands, for she was a mere servant and in his employ and everything she touched belonged to him, including her own body, she was the one who had risked the siege and the starved children and the dangerous hungry men who might have been in the street; she was the one who had built the fire and peeled the roots and made the soup. And she felt within herself an angry understanding that her rights in this matter were superior to his.

And so she poured out all that was left within the kettle into the bowl, and staring grimly at him, she drank that down as well.

He could not shout at her without bringing notice that the family had eaten hot food when no one else all around had had a mouthful for days. And so he, who was smooth and mild and never violent back in the city across the ocean, did rise from his bed and loom over the girl and punch her in the stomach with all his might, for it was in the rights of the master of the house to punish the women and servants within.

She bent over, heaving, fighting to breathe and keep her hard-won food within her, as the master hunched over the kettle and scraped out the burnt bits with his spoon.

And here, in her stony cleft beside the river, after the first bite of the fish's flesh, the girl's shrunken stomach protested, she leapt to her feet and vomited the chewed flesh out onto the bare rock, where it froze in an instant. Then she sat back down within her warm dark place and cut another slice from the fish and she tried it again. She breathed through the coldness of this bite upon her tongue until she could swallow, she breathed some more until the food settled. She fed the fire more sticks to allow her stomach to start to work, and in this hotter glow, in her patience, she began to remember what it was to eat. The sheets of flesh melted faster, peeled off the thawing fish thicker, went down more easily.

And there the fish in bites sat inside her, and there inside it stayed.

4.

Slowly through the afternoon she ate the fish, and when she had eaten down to the bones of one side, she flipped it over and it seemed whole again, if strangely tailless.

But as soon as she flipped it, a miracle of renewal, the now-thawed fish upon the ground gave a kick of its tail stub. Its mouth gaped silent, then closed again. It had been half stripped of its body and yet, it appeared, the fish was still alive.

In horror, she brought the flat end of the hatchet down hard and beat the creature into a more certain death. The eye that had rekindled clouded over. Then she peeled the flesh from the second side of the fish, and, fighting sickness, ate the rest.

She ate the fish's sweet cheeks; she ate its brain. The eyes that stared at her, appalled, she ate last.

She fetched more dry branches to feed the fire, she drank the cold water, she shat in a hot loose flood because she hadn't contained anything within her body to shit out in weeks, and now her own body was re-awakening. Such reawakenings are raw. The nerves in the ends of her fingers and lips were afire. Her belly was distended, the skin painfully stretched, like that of a gravid woman near to the time of childbirth.

When she'd sucked the fish bones dry and cast them out onto the rocks for the crows that had watched her in the trees, she lay back near her fire and felt her own well-being nearly overwhelm her with its sweet flood, its goodness. She was warm enough now, her clothing had dried, the fish's flesh was melting into her own, she was far from the bitterness of the fort.

She slept through the remainder of the afternoon and woke with crampings in her stomach so heavy that she was sweating, and just in time, she scrabbled out onto the rocks, into the trees, and lifted her skirts, feeling the entirety of her guts heaving themselves out of her body.

It was there as she crouched in her pain that she understood that in her sleep she had come to a decision about what she must do. Perhaps the fish that was thrashing out of her guts was the thing that had made her decision for her. She would cross the frozen river. She would risk the rotten ice.

She took herself and the hatchet back to the hole in the ice where she had dug out the top half of the fish, and hacked out the tail still embedded there. She put it in her sack to keep for later.

Back in the hovel, she replaced the cup, hatchet, knife, flint, and two coverlets in the sack, lifted her cape and gowns, and retied the sack next to the skin of her waist. Without the coverlets to keep the fire's warmth close, she felt the cold seep into her again.

She waited until the day went full black to night again and the moon rose nearly whole, then she came out of her little hovel in the rocks and crouched on the edge of the flat plain of green-white ice, feeling the way her body was pinched tight in her fear. There would be no sense in staying, she would be unlikely to find more food around here and could not know if anyone was following, although something in her spoke quietly and urgently and said that she was in fact being followed and that her pursuer was nearing. If she was going to go, she must go now, as the river would soon become impossible to cross with the coming melt.

In the bare light from the moon, the ice looked thick and welcoming, but ice was deceptive when covered with snow, and at the tail of winter, rivers went brittle, and she was sure there were places out there that could not bear her weight.

If she were to step upon ice so thin that she would go through and be sucked down into the frigid currents, well, perhaps it was not for the worst, for a sailor on the ship across the ocean had told her that drowning was a friendlier way to die than most dying was. There would be, he had said while wrapping a rope around his arm tattooed in roses, at first a knifelike terror and a panicking, a thrashing of all the limbs, but then the cold would steal all the motion from the body and the lungs would take water inside, and though there might be a painful first choking, a stillness would come over the self, a pause, and life would ebb out and the soul would drift toward the sun.

And she had believed him, for he had heard all this from a man who had gone overboard in a storm in the North Sea and the man had drowned to death and had returned to life only when they'd pushed his legs into his belly a hundred times and pumped a fire-bellows into his rectum until the water came out of him and the air could come in again.

It was not sad to her, this idea of the river gathering her dead body up into its dark hands and carrying it bumping under the ice all the way down into the great bay, where the larger and more vicious fish would find her and eat her up, just as she had eaten the fish that thrashed within her guts now. With delight, these huge fish would strip the flesh off her bones, and thrust their heads into her viscera, and let the knobs of her spine fall from their mouths and be buried by the muck at the bottom of the bay. She preferred the fishes to the worms of the earth, for fish were a higher form of life. There would be poetry in the repetition: fish into girl, girl into fish. Perhaps the eternal chain of being was not a chain at all but a ring, one life not ending where the other begins but all souls overlapping.

For, on the other side of life, she would rejoin the child Bess, who was alone now in the valley of death, only her father the goldsmith there to greet her and the impersonal angels to wait upon her, to tie her latchets and brush her long hair and keep her fingers out of her nostrils. The child Bess, who, in her idiocy and gentleness, was as trusting as a kitten and would curl into any warm body that embraced her, was always certain of love, and she would weep fat tears if the angels in their business and cold perfection would recoil from her need.

The girl took a step onto the ice. The river stretched a pale enormity, made ever vaster by her fear. One foot tenderly outstretched before she put it down, then the next. She listened for cracks, she felt for softness beneath. But soon, with the bolts of terror that struck and rocked her, she began to shuffle and then to slide into a run.

And now she saw herself as she often did in heightened moments, as though from the air, like a hovering bird or the moon itself. She saw herself a black and creeping thing across the slick greenish surface of the ice, the snow crystals glistening and catching and throwing shards of moonlight.

Once, she felt the heel of her left boot going through the fine surface of ice, touching the water of the river beneath, but she was already in the air toward the next footstep and this second landed solid and held, and she ran faster; knowing how close she had come to plunging into the river, she flew, and speed and fear had become her sails.

At last, she felt the pebbles of the far shore under her feet and the solid rock beneath her, and she let herself stop and breathe raggedly. She clutched to herself the first tree she came to, pressed her face to it, and laughed. She had put the treacherous river between herself and the darkness that she had fled; she laughed because she found herself fully alive.

The tree she held smelled of sweetness and musk and the sap stirring deep within its rings, for the tree knew it would be spring quite soon and that out of this white sleep there would arise the greenness of new life.

And she would be not very far away at all when the blank sheet of river ice would break up all at once.

She would not see it shatter but would hear it as she moved through the forest, the boom of the breaking ice. And she would imagine an avalanche, a rockslide of stones falling into a gorge, perhaps even thunder from a storm that raged invisibly in the clouds.

Now she moved carefully up the night-dark bank into the trees and spent some time simply listening, turning her face up because she was smelling some faint familiar note on the wind.

When she understood that what she smelled was the smoke of a village of the people of this place, she hurried back down to the riverbank and crept along there as quietly as she could until, when she stopped and lifted her nose and tried to trace the scent of smoke to sense if the village was still near, all she could smell was winter and ice and mud, and she believed she had left the village behind her.

Soon she came upon a break in the woods that showed itself to be a path away from the river to the north. She did not know that this path ran past the far edge of the village. When she walked it, all the dogs curled together in the burying grounds lifted their heads and went still and focused, listening to the girl's movements along the borders of their kingdom, and each dog weighed its alarm against the sounds of the creature out there moving swiftly along, and each decided the creature was too slight to be of danger, each decided to hold its bark until the strange beast departed and the night in its wake poured back in, full of its ordinary sounds.

She followed this path for a stretch of moonlight, climbing a hill. At the top, she stopped and turned and saw the vines of smoke from the sleeping village as they climbed toward the sky, and below the smoke there was the long snaking shining skin of the river that she had crossed.

She turned away, back toward the path, and went on, and only moments later, the soldier who had been sent from the fort came into the clearing on the far side of the frozen water, at the very place where the stream that the girl had followed emptied out into the river.

The man wore a musket on his back and knives at his belt. He was a grim and savage man who struck fear in the hearts of any who knew him, not for his appearance, which was plain and quite unremarkable, with fresh and rosy cheeks and a tiny pursed mouth, but because of the look he bore in his eyes like a wild creature that had scented blood and gone out of its head for wanting. He was the one chosen to hunt down the murderess servant who had run away, because, the men of the fort said of him, he did not know mercy. Or perhaps, they muttered well out of his hearing, it was because he did not fear god.

He saw the girl's bootprints in the moonlight as they trailed to her hovel in the stone. There, he crouched down, feeling with his fingers the warmth of where she had laid her fire, and touching the ashes for freshness, and seeing the scattering of bones and scales, and smelling the fatty fish smell, which made him hungrier. The stone crevice held some scent, he imagined, that came from the girl's skin and the pouch of strong sweet herbs she wore on a thong around her neck as defense against the rancid stink of death in the fort. He had seen the girl, had been biding his time until he could find her alone. Now he dipped his head to the space that had held her body, and licked the warm stone.

They had called the servant girl a fool in the fort, but she was no fool; she was perhaps smart, he thought, looking at what she had managed, food and shelter in so harsh a clime. He followed her footsteps to the edge of the ice and saw them stretch boldly marked in the snow and moonlight far across the river. Perhaps she had fallen in, perhaps she had made it all the way across. He could see that the surface of the ice was not steady, that there were darker spots where it had rotted, and he did not trust ice, for he knew it to be a liar. He had already risked his own neck enough to follow the girl through the siege. And there was no telling that ice that could hold a slip of a girl would hold a man twice her size.

There would be no boats for weeks, not until the ice melted and broke up and the water was passable; and he would lose weeks in the wilderness if he were to follow the river until it narrowed and he could safely make it across in chase of this nothing, this starved murderess of a girl.

Pity, he thought. For he had savored the fantasy of squeezing the murderess's throat until she went black and was dead in his hands. Once, in the city, he had squeezed the throat of a whore until she stopped kicking and her breath stopped and her eyes bulged, and he had since longed to do it again, he had so loved the strength in his hands and the feel of her windpipe as it collapsed. It took a tremendous amount of strength to strangle a woman to death, it was not a sport of the weak. Yes, a true pity that he would not do it again now, there was so little opportunity in this place to satisfy his bleaker urges, the raids against the men of the land were often bloody, but there is a difference between private violence and violence to fight for a foothold in this place. One could be taken out in private, savored, the other was a godly duty.

Instead, he must return and report the girl dead of falling through the river, drowned, which she likely had done. It mattered little. He spat through the missing teeth on the left side of his mouth and curled down into the small hole where the girl had been, for it was still warm in there from her fire and her body and out of the wind, and there he slept fitfully through the end of the night. He knew he should wait until daylight had died again and night was full upon him, but to induce him on this mission, the governor, who still had some small flour left, had promised him bread, which he had not tasted in months, and he would give nearly anything to taste bread again, hot bread, he longed for it, and he thought he could make it back to the fort in the daylight alive. He doubled back with long strides over the miles he had covered in chase of the girl and killed a weasel and built a small fire and cooked the weasel in the spanish way, stripped of its skin and threaded upon a stick and roasted over the flames. So fortified, he would have made it back even in his mission's failure, which had been to bring the girl to her punishment, living or dead, for her body would have been trussed nude and hanged upon the high palisade as warning to others. But then not far from the fort, the men of the powhatan suddenly emerged out of the woods surrounding him. And he knew some of them from his own earlier violence and the raids that he had taken a bloody ecstatic relish in, laughing as he killed. And even while raising the musket, he understood that he was already a dead man.

And though the girl was nowhere near the soldier when he had imagined strangling her to death, something malignant in his thought sent its tendrils through space and they reached the girl and made the cold shoot upward from the small of her back through her spine, they caused her to look around wildly and break into a trot up the incline that she was walking.

For what woman has not, walking in the dark of the street or along a path deep in the countryside, sensed the brutal imaginings of a man watching her from his hidden place, and felt the same chills chasing over her skin, and quickened her steps to get away.

If the river had put a barrier between herself and the men of the fort, she knew, though she tried not to think of it, that it did not protect her from the men of the lands here, who could be everywhere, who could be watching her now. She shook. Her fear of these men was the fear of the unknown, for she had seen very little of them, only once in the autumn when the powhatan had been grudging friends of the fort. A bright and laughing girl of theirs, rumored to be a daughter of the powhatan king, had come with her servants bearing gifts of venison and baskets of corn, and she was so energetic a girl, so delighted in herself, that she had dared the boys of the fort to turn cartwheels and had cartwheeled behind them with her gleeful nakedness, with the long braided lock at the back of her razed head whipping all about. And the minister, the mistress's husband, had watched from the door of the church, and when he felt his wife's sardonic eye watching him watch the girl, he had flushed red and hissed, For shame that wanton creature shows her privies off to the eyes of men.

And the mistress, whose tongue had always been a dagger, had said, O for shame thou lookest upon the privies of a child.

And the minister sputtered and went still, and after a long silence, he laughed also, for still at the beginning of the long dark winter there had remained a vein of gold in him.

It was behind the shoulders of the master and mistress that the girl had looked with wonder upon the free child, at the young strong bearers of the food, each one wearing a side of his head shaved and clubs upon his waist and some tattoos upon his face, and one even who kept a yellow snake as a pet and wore an earring threaded in his ear. And though the girl from inside the church had felt a ravenous curiosity and had wanted to sidle near the young men, they were gone nearly as soon as they had come. And she remained ignorant of them save what she had been told.

When relations with the people of the powhatan began to sour, there soon rose rumors of their dark doings, for it struck fear in the settlers' hearts to be among enemies who were far larger in number than the english and who understood the land far better and had customs cloaked in shadow. They were unknown and were therefore strange. These rumors rippled outward and redoubled back to the girl's ears in waves of terror, so that the stories she had overheard or been told in the morning always returned to her by evening to be retold infinitely worse.

For one, she reflected as she walked so fast that she may as well have been running, was the tale of the soldier whose head was cleaved from his body and bread stuffed into his mouth as if in mockery of the gnawing famine that all the settlers suffered.

For another, the many tales of the men who had to creep back to the fort from raids or trading excursions, pressing their hands to their crowns to stanch the blood pouring out, for their hair and flesh had been ripped off to the bone of the skull.

For yet another, and the worst, was one that belonged to the first wave of settlers, when the gentlemen who had come had refused to dirty their hands with the hard necessary work and the soldiers were lusty for treasure and did nothing but search for gold, which they did not find. In this godless time, there had been a soldier who had come across one of the powhatan girls in the forest and, starved to madness for the company of women, had pushed the girl down and had his way with her body as she screamed and wept, and when he had used her, he left her lying there in the dirt bleeding. Some time passed, then one day, when this same man was out in the bay gathering oysters, he looked up to find that his companions were nowhere near him, that they had disappeared as if they had been told to flee, and even the birds in the trees had silenced themselves and were waiting. Then, as though magicked out of the fog that lay upon the waters, women began to take shape all around him and came close and had him surrounded in silence. Before he could cry out, they put a leather thong in his mouth so that he was muted and could not scream, then they dragged him away with them by the hair of his head, and in that same night, four women tied him as naked as a newborn babe to the twinned trees visible from the gate of the fort, the man's arms and legs wrenched outspread and his body stretched to the near snapping of his joints. Then they built a fire in front of him so that his pale skin was glowing against the dark behind him, and they loosed the thong in his mouth so that his screams could be heard even into the heart of the fort. Then all at once, more women poured out of the forest with sharpened oyster shells in their hands. With these as their knives, the women slowly flayed the skin off the man, first his eyelids so that he had no choice but to watch what they were doing to him. Next, the skin of his arms and legs and his belly, all of which they threw into the fire before his peeled eyes. Then they removed the tongue from his mouth so that, though he could no longer speak words and pray to his god, he could yet scream through the clotting pouring blood. Then they removed his privy members. They took the figs first, then the manhood. At this, at last, he lost his senses entirely, and they waited for him to wake again, singing and laughing, before they made him watch as they threw his useless male parts upon the spitting devouring fire. Only then in mercy did they slit his throat and let the hot blood pour out to steam upon the ground.

This had been told in hushed breath as evidence of the godlessness within the people of this place, but the girl's thoughts had already snagged and held upon an earlier atrocity, upon the girl of the people of this place who had been held to the earth and outraged; it was as if she herself could feel the dirt in her own mouth, the press of the man's heavy body upon her bones, for this brutality of the bodies of men, she, herself, did know.

And likewise, while the men of the fort whispered and spoke these stories of fear, there was a part of the girl that resisted, that sang in low counterpoint, reminding her of the bridge over the river in the city of her birth and the way the enemies of the late queen had had their heads stuck aloft on pikes, their beards flapping in a hard wind and their mouths open in death so it seemed that they were silently screaming. And all the while beneath this vaunting of death, the carts heavy with their vegetables, their turnips and their cabbages, rolled serenely on, and the farmers thought of the beer and bread awaiting them and took no notice of these horrid tokens of death.

For, verily, godlessness and murder, the girl knew, were certainly not limited to the people of this new country.

It was also the case that, when the women and the children of the fort disappeared during the long abject famine, the men of the council said angrily that the men of the place had swept through silent and invisible as the wind and had stolen them. But the girl had always wondered if it wasn't so, if perhaps the cleverest of the women, seeing the danger on both sides and weighing it, had taken up their children and fled out to the life of the others, perhaps even if it meant being used hard as slaves. For it was a truth that mothers, having already lost their liberty when they bore children, having been tethered to the earth with this new soft tender body they must now protect forever, were the ones who understood the delicate balance between the price of freedom and the price of their children's lives.

There had been a time in the child Bess's deepest sufferings of refusal that the girl herself had nearly decided to do the same, to heave her beloved child onto her small back and flee with her away from the fort to try to save her slender life.

And yet further was a shame so deep that it could not be admitted in the open, but it was commonly known and whispered about that some of the men of the other peoples, those who knew the land and watched the fort and besieged the english on the side of the powhatan, had been born to names like John and Peter and Richard, born to the knowledge of churchbells and the din of horses and carts upon cobbled streets. That these men had been englishmen who had fled the fort when the settlers started dying, that they had turned from the light of god and consigned their souls to the devil in desperate bargain to keep their bodies alive. It was said that these apostate englishmen knew with intimacy the weaknesses of their own kind and the paltry extent of their stores, and did barter this knowledge in exchange for their lives.

5.

When the stars were out, their light fell upon the earth with nearly the strength of the sun on a dim day, and the girl walked northward on the path carved out of light and shadow.

In time, the girl wondered what feet were the ones that created this path, and she imagined the men of this country in their quiet steady passage through the forest. She became frightened and replaced the men in her mind with the feet of deer, a doe and her new trembling fawn. In so doing, she calmed herself.

She felt excellent in her joints tonight, excellent in her bones, and under her skin, her blood rushed strong within her. Her boots were sturdy and dry, and they carried her onward, and within her thick hooded cloak, her body was warm. Night creatures rustled in the trees without caring that she was passing beneath them. A happiness of her strong body and her solitude overcame her, and she was glad to be where she was in this bright clear crystal night.

Later, as she moved quietly along, she came to a stream bank where the ice had withdrawn to show bare stone and found two great racks of antlers interlaced and shining whitely in the starlight.

Inscribed clear into the tangled antlers was a story of the mute and furious struggle that had taken place, the two deer that had charged across the earth and hit with a loud noise and become locked together so that even when they had lost their strength and given up their anger they could not separate. Then each did fall to his knees conjoined with his enemy and gave up his breath in the company of the one he hated.

The antlers were enormous, pale and shadow-struck upon the gray stone, so huge that she stopped in her swift passage to gaze upon them. Her breath quieted in her, and her body that had been startled out of its forward motion hummed. No sculpture, no painting, no tapestry made by the hands of man had yet caused in her such a torrent of feeling. She stared at the antlers until she felt them seared into her, so that she could later imagine them upon the back of her eyelids when she wanted to summon a surge of melancholy. But soon her body cooled until she was uncomfortable, and to warm herself again, she moved on.

As the night ended, there grew from the earth a pale mist that enveloped first her ankles then her knees then her waist then her chest then the entirety of her person, and soon it blacked out the light of the stars and the new day being born at the edge of the east. The mist carried a wicked and clammy cold that slid up against her skin and made her gasp. Her shaking grew more pronounced and she became loud to herself. If she was loud to herself, she knew, she would be loud to whatever ears of beast or man were nearby.

The path had obscured itself in the foul curtain of mist, and her boots stumbled against the roots and stones she could not see. What tree branches and trunks showed themselves did so only as she was about to strike them with her face. If she went onward like this, she could easily stumble off the side of a cliff or look up to find that she was standing at the center of a village of the people of this place who might not wish her well, who might trade her back to the fort and thus ensure her death.

And so she stopped where she was, and with her hands in their gloves extended, she felt her way into the trees. And finding a place that was flat and free of snow, she knelt and tried to make a fire of whatever dry matter came to hand. But in this wet exhalation from the thawing earth, all that she touched was wet as well, all the bark and branches and leaves and moss she found, and she could feel no dead sticks on the trees that she could strip and set alight. The sparks she caused to fly from the flint leapt into the air and the damp pinched them out.

She failed and failed and failed some more, and soon, her body having stopped in its warming forward motion, the cold pushed itself ever deeper into her, and she gasped at it, for it was terrible.

At last, she felt her way on her hands and knees on the ground, and discovered a flat rock held against a tree, or a tree growing into a rock, it was hard to discern which, and she pulled her two coverlets from the sack and with one made as much of a tent as she could with two crotched sticks that she had cut from the tree above. She pulled the other coverlet tight against her body but the cold wormed its way in and the rock beneath her radiated its cold upward and into her bones. She was wretched. And though she was infinitely weary, sleep would not come to her.

This was a lesson, she told herself, that she had learned along with her pain, that she must gather what dry plant stuff and sticks she passed in the day and stow them away in her sack for when she was too weary to go on. For she could have no comfort in these unfriendly woods without the heat from fire; and without fire, her body lay exposed to the more perilous beasts that might scent her and draw near.

She drifted into a half-dreaming slumber. Soon there rose the impression that the ground beneath her was not solid like good firm land but was buckling and shifting as if she had been carried in her sleep back to the ship, which even in the doldrums still moved and swayed and was imperfectly steady underfoot, changeable as the waves and currents beneath it.

From the beginning, when they were still tethered to the docks in the city, she had loved this swing of the water. And later, as they went out into the larger waves, she had been one of the very few to find herself at peace in her stomach. She cared for the others as they retched and vomited and panted and groaned in their agonies, as their bodies thinned, unable to take in food. In any event, even if they had been able, the food was impossible, mostly half-cooked messes of worm-riddled peas.

Mayhap there is some salt in your blood, my dear Lamentations, the mistress murmured from under the girl's soothing hand upon her hot forehead. Mayhap we have solved one of the mysteries of your parentage. And she laughed, not unkindly. For it was true that the girl had come out of the parish poorhouse into the mistress's household at four years of age or thereabouts; she had been discovered a newborn babe, all alone one bad dawn, still in the juices of birth, and naked in the filth of shiteburne lane, and nearly dead of cold.

The mistress had wondered at this, at what mother could be so wretched to give birth in such a filthy place, what mother could be so desperate to leave her child there to die? Only, the mistress said with a pretense of sadness, a whore. And as she was a woman of fantasy and imagination, she summoned in a few phrases the life of such a creature, godless and alone, brought on a ship from some far place, knowing nobody, perhaps speaking none of the english language but the most vile phrases, stealing out from the stew where she had been kept in the darkest dankest corner of the city only to squat in the street and weep her baby into the world. And the mistress was gifted with such a tongue that it seemed to the girl to be the likely truth and that there was one of her parents surely accounted for.

For the other, her father, the girl liked this new idea that he had been a seafarer, for this might explain her skin far darker than saxon or celtic or norman skin and her dark hair and her dark eyes. Even upon the *Blessing*, the ship carrying them to the new world, there had been sailors who had been born portuguese and moorish and even a small sunbrowned man whose face was not so very unlike the one the girl had seen when she stared into her mistress's glass. But unlike his, hers was, as the other servants and the mistress's artist friends told her, delicate and pretty and flushed a rose pink in the cheeks. She was rightfully vain of the impression it made and of her good strong dancing body.

———

There on the ship, while all about her people slept fitful sleep, she felt long days of peace for the first time in her life. She, accustomed to constant business and bustle, had only to care for her household, and she had time to fly to the upper decks for air, for all below was as sour and befouled and dank as the worst wretchedness of hell. When the wind was fine, she stayed perched out of the way of the sailors working and stared at the blue immensity and felt a deep wonder surging in her. In the night, she loved to watch the wide track of the moon upon the pleated water and the strange creatures she saw or imagined that surfaced to stare upon the passing boat. She loved the taste of the wind, all salt, and kept her mouth open to let it in.

And one night, in the quiet up on the deck, she was wrapped in a coverlet against the sharpish wind and dreaming when she became aware of a man who had come close to her in silence and was now sitting not far from her. She looked across at him and he looked back, hiding his mouth because his teeth were bad, although his face was good, shy and large-cheeked and crinkling at the outside corners of his eyes. He was a dutchman, large and silent, his english small, and he was not much older than she was, still a boy but strong in his man's body. He had trained as a glassblower, he told her in motions of his hands, and showed her the slick of a scar running wrist to elbow from burning glass, or so she assumed. She touched the scar, and under her fingers, it felt smooth at the center and puckered at the edges. She slowly put her mouth to it and licked. He put his large hands to her cheeks, and one hand moved down her body over her clothes and came to rest in the space between her legs that had felt a shock, a pleasureful rush. And then she came closer toward him and the smell of him thrilled her, and soon she found herself held up against the wall, her haunches in his hands, her skirts up, and he within them. She laughed in surprise because she found with him, his strong shoulders under her arms, a yearning here, a liquid agitation that made her feel both strong and weak, and this was strange to her, unforeseen, because before this night upon the boat, the same frenzied act threatened upon her resisting form had held only a dry brittle panic and a swift chute into resignation then the spit upon the palm and the girl closing her eyes, knowing that the doors were closed, the household gone deaf to her so that even if she cried out there could be no unsealing of ears to hear her. This was not that, not in the least. This was good. Her body felt large. The boy smiled into her cheek, she could feel the crinkles of the skin beside his eyes, she was delighted. She bit his shoulder. She cracked the boy like a nut between her teeth and found him savory meat.

He finished, and though there was something building within her that wanted him longer, that seemed close enough to her own version of his gasp and buckle, she did not arrive at it that night, and she did not mind. And later, during the long days of sailing ever westward with the bright hard wind and the pods of dolphins following the boat, she scrambled to finish her chores for the family, the running and fetching and cleaning and caring so that she could steal away toward where the craftsman dutchboys sat on their corner of the deck and catch a glimpse of his hair so pale that it shone like water. And she felt a similar light shining though her; she liked him even more when she could see him and he could look blushing at her, though during the day they could not touch.

She was drunk, she thought, with the hidden powers of her own body, which she had never much regarded as anything but the dancing and singing and fetching tool it had been. With this tender unfurling light within her, even the minister, whom she had learned to hate so deep, had begun to cast again to her eyes the dazzling rays he had radiated off him in the city when she had sat beside her mistress watching him preach in the church in the months before he wedded himself to her. For though he hid his vanity and his avid hungers behind the shallow prettiness of his face the way a lazy plasterer hides the rot of the wall behind a white surface skim, there was also an unconscious charm in the minister that rose to meet women from whom he felt a warmth of love.

And though the girl listened with two ears, her wiser ear still hating him, she let his prayers and sermons on the boat comfort and fill her, and he, sensing a softening in her, smiled on her with his good teeth and face of surpassing beauty. And as all upon the boat was more beautiful to her than the life in the city, even this hatred was abated and a new uncertain kindness lay between them.

One night, the glassblower pressed something like a ball into her hand, which felt springy to her fingers, and when she put it to her nose, she gasped, for she smelled that he had given her an orange. She had known oranges and lemons in the city, rare treats. He laughed at the girl's pleasure and took the fruit from her hand and carefully with his knife peeled it, then pressed a slice into her mouth. It tasted the way her body felt with him. He put his face close and licked the juice from her chin. She kissed his nose. He said something in his language. She understood without understanding the words and said, You are dear to me, also. She put a handslength of peel in her bodice, and when she bent in the day to work, she smelled the orange and her body flushed and the bones of her hips felt liquid.

When she fell asleep pressed to the warmth of the child Bess, who upon the boat was still speaking, smiling, laughing, the girl fell asleep dreaming of her glassblower. In her dreams, they had a house in some pretty place in the new world and acres of their own land thickly growing all around. It was neat with the neatness of all her work and lit by good candles and firelight, and upon the table she laid a great plenty of food. And her bed was warmed by his body. O let it be, she thought, or even let it be a hovel dark and drear, her single dress grown ratted and filthy, the food sparse, as long as this boy was with her, he would be shelter and warmth and meat in her belly.

But a day came when the edge of the sky began to boil, and the waves grew ever larger until they each became the size of a goodly hill. The boat tipped drunkenly from side to side. In the high blowing wind, the rain came down with such thickness it seemed a river cascading from the clouds, the air so full of water that a body could not breathe without taking water into the lungs.

Then the hills of the waves became mountains. The deck was abandoned to the elements. In the hold, where the people and the beasts languished, the lanterns blew out; the days of darkness, the days of true misery, began.

The waves crashed and the wind screamed, and what noise there was outside was matched by the prayers and shouts within.

When the boat drew itself up the side of each vastness of water, those who were not already too weak or yet dead clutched the nets in the bulwarks and held on. Then there was the terrible pause at the top, long enough to consider all the sins and horrors and disappointments that the soul had absorbed in its stretch of life so far. There in the pause, the knowledge of what was to come made them weep aloud in terror. Then, with a sickening lurch, the boat broke away and fell down down down down down, and screams rose before all air was squeezed from the lungs and into the voiceless silence, all objects left stupidly unsecured at the start of the storm went flying, the buckets in which vomit had been caught, and chamberpots likewise and worse, and spoons and wet books flapping as swift as bats and small trunks and a suckling babe fallen from its mother's arms, now stiff and cold, and the larger bodies of the unsecured dead. And as it was near total black inside the hold when such loose things in falling struck the bodies of the living, it was as a whip falling upon them or a fist wakening them from a good sleep, and they would sob in their torments like piteous children again. Then the boat would crash down into the bottom of the troughs, and the planks would scream as if about to break, and the filthy water would pour all over them. Each heart would pray that this would be the moment of smashing up, that the sea would at last rush in and snatch all the souls out of this immensity of agony and deliver them into the blackness of death beyond, for they did not believe that they could survive yet another long drawing up the mountains of the waves and another fearsome falling. But they did.

Rather, most did. And the living suffered for an infernal three days without rest. Since the time when the waves were mere hills, the girl had tied herself with ropes around the child Bess, who was too weak to cling to the netting and would have had no will to do so. With her own strong body, the girl kept the child Bess from being flung from one side of the hold to the other and breaking her neck. Though the girl felt broken all through her body by the time the waves calmed, they were both still alive. The child Bess's hair in her mouth, tasting of lavender and milk, the feel of the child's trembling body warm against her own, was the only solid truth in the swirling darkness, and perhaps even the only thing that kept the girl herself among the living. In the thick of the torment, she prayed for her glassblower and longed for him; but he, being away from her in the urgency of the torment, had become distant from her, a memory of another life.

At the end of the third day of such hell, the world soothed itself. The waves were merely large hills to climb and tumble down, then they were small hills, then they brushed against the boat and did not rock it hard. The girl was so sore and exhausted that when she was untied she felt nearly dead. The child Bess mewled and fat tears fell down her cheeks and she slobbered on her own hand in her mouth to comfort herself.

The survivors dragged themselves up to the sunlight on the deck, their flesh battered black and blue, many bones broken, all in an immensity of pain. Not a soul had been left untouched by the storm, and all had bargained with god in their hearts to relinquish pride and vanity and greed if they could survive this depth of terror. But the promises so seared into their flesh would fade as the storm faded away, as the bruises diminished and the bones knit whole again, and they would go on as the sinners they had always been.

The girl, having carried the child Bess to the fresh air and returned to be the staff supporting first the mistress then the minister to the deck, rose to her feet and took herself through the groaning bodies, searching for her glassblower. But she could not find him. At last, she came near the cluster of boys that he had been among, pale exhausted dutchboys who had the bodies of men but still the minds of boys, and with what bits of the language she had picked up from her own dutch-boy and the motions of her hands, she asked them where he was. And they looked up doleful and blushing, some with shining tears in their eyes, and told her as well as they could that their friend had gone up on deck at the beginning of the storm when the waves were not so severe, that he had been seeking the girl, and that nobody had seen him since.

She knew from this that her boy had been washed off the face of the ship. And then he had been frantic alone in the black swelling water, bobbing up the sheer rise of the waves before one had swallowed him, had held him under, and he had breathed the darkness into him and he had drowned. The beautiful body that she had so delighted in, the beautiful dream of a house, and fields, and children, was gone with him to the very bottom of the ocean, food for the sharks and the fishes.

For some time then, the girl went quiet and very still. She did no longer sing. She spent her days among the other servant girls scrubbing and washing and laundering all that had become so filthy during the storm, which was everything. They paused in their scrubbing only to help

stitch up the shrouds of those who had died. Then they stood in a sor-
rowing ring around the corpses, listening to the minister, the mistress's
husband, as he gave a short eulogy, then the sailors tipped the corpses
out to the circling sharks. Noblemen had died and servants had died;
death did not see rank but came for all. It must be said that the minister
wept truly for these departed souls. Though the girl had learned to hate
him full, for this time of mourning on the boat she wept alongside
of him, feeling her grief lessened by his grief and that of the other
mourners.

Then the bruit rose up that, at the end of the storm—when what men
who could stagger and crawl, even the governor and the younger
brothers of earls and the surgeon and the captain, the gentlemen who
could not be expected to work, had all been engaged in trying to pump
and bail the water that was seeping in through the hull—someone had
looked up to the top of the mast to see a small ball of light leaping merrily all about it. And it was whispered that the light was the ghost of a
soul whose body had perished of terror during the storm. Everyone
who had lost a person, the mothers of the dead babes and the friends of
the drowned and broken-necked, believed this soul to be their own beloved returned to proffer comfort to the ones they had left.

For some time, the girl considered the likeliness that the ball of light
had been the glassblower. But she remembered his modesty and gentleness, and thought that it could not be so, for a ball of light was a vaunting drama indeed. When his soul left his body, it ascended directly
through the storm and came to rest at the right hand of god, she knew.

————

Though the bodies of the dead occupied them, as did clearing away the filth of terror, the worst loss had occurred to them when the survivors had brought themselves, nearly destroyed, to the deck and had looked in all four directions and had found that the other ships were missing. There was no worse aloneness than to see no other sign of civilization in the watery wastes. They believed the other ships lost to the sea monsters, only the *Blessing* remaining in the light of the sun. And even those who had clung ferocious to life during the three days of the storm despaired and longed for death.

It was with rejoicing then that in the afternoon on the first day of terrifying solitude, over the distance came the *Falcon*, then the *Lion*, then the *Unitie*. All had suffered losses. In their sad flotilla, they lurched sick over the last stretch of ocean.

At last, there appeared in the waters the detritus of land: clusters of seaweed tangled with sticks and leaves, and seabirds began flying over them that were of the bigness of pigeons. And then they saw the land itself, a darkness scribbled against the horizon that grew green as they neared, that seemed a true paradise, verdant rich. They fell to their knees and gave passionate thanks. Closer to land, they saw purple and pink and green birds flitting, and the trees were immense, straight and stern and tall, and were hung with vines. Closest, the seabirds screamed with such familiarity that they sounded like the seagulls on the wharf in the city back home.

They limped up the bay, the four remaining boats, and with the last of their forces, they found themselves finally where they had meant to go, the settlement upon the river James, named after their king.

But there the smoke lay upon the fort thick and hideous, and the men who came out to gape at them were pale skeletons on the bank. There was more smoke rising from the men's hungry mouths, tobacco smoked to stave off the pangs of their starvation, for the famine was already taking root.

On the deck, the girl stood beside her mistress, looking down upon the men's weakness and sickness, their faces showing their obvious dismay at the sight of the ships bringing no true relief, only more hungry mouths to feed.

The mistress, who had aged considerably upon the ship, or who had let down her artifices so her true age showed clear, said, aghast and her lips pale, We have made a terrible mistake in coming here.

In days and weeks, there sailed into the river some of the remaining boats that had been assumed lost forever: the *Diamond*, the *Swallow*, much later the *Virginia*. And though it was good that less had been lost than all had feared, still it was a pity, they all said, that the two ships with nearly all the comestibles and most of the obvious leaders lay storm-smashed in pieces upon the bottom of the ocean.

Even now in the knit and purl of mist that made the girl shudder, even as the ground seemed to be breathing as though she were a flea and it the breast of a giant, even within the scope of all that she had lost, which was nearly everything, the thought of the voyage out to the new world suffused her with an awful sorrow. She mourned all that they had suffered together but mostly her own private loss of the glass-blower. What he had been in his own beautiful body and what he had meant to her dreams. All the sturdy bright-haired new-world children they would have made had vanished with him, and the acres of meadow that they would have bought or taken from the people of this place and plowed and planted and defended and built into a kingdom of their own she would never touch with her own hands in this life. She growing old as the proud mother of strong boys. Love enough for a lifetime. All gone.

Then this phantom second self blew through her and rose out of her and dispersed into the mist that swallowed her on the cold ground, and she was left alone on the wobbling earth again.

6.

The sun, she knew, had risen, because the mist began to change. Now it revealed the outline of her hand at a few inches' distance from her face. Her own body became a ghostly apparition fading in and out of view.

Warmth was seeping into the world now, the low mist catching the rays of the sun and cupping the heat within it.

All around, there rose a pattering sound that alarmed her, so like it was to the feet of many thousands of animals moving through the forest, and she thought in fear of a stampede of something tiny and swift, something ratlike, a flood of rats pouring over her. Then she understood when a drop of water ran down the vertical branch of her coverlet-tent and dripped upon her forehead that the day had warmed enough to melt the snow that was still in the trees, that the drops of snowmelt were falling to the earth in a rain.

Her outside coverlet had absorbed the wet. She was thirsty, so she squeezed the edges of the coverlet into her pewter cup, and fished the insects from it with a clean twig, and drank the woolly water down.

There would be no rest in this morning with all the wetness, she knew. And though the night had bruised her deeper into her long fatigue, she rose to her feet, wobbling a little and groaning in the pain. She packed her things into the sack and was about to feel her way to the path through the woods when there was a commotion near her. There before her, spinning around a tree trunk, she saw a furious squirrel shouting and clicking its teeth and threatening her with its plush tail. She felt her way around the tree until she saw just above her head the black hole of its nest. She pushed her hand in and brought out five squirming pink baby squirrels, which she killed one by one by spitting them on the knife, then sliding the small bodies onto a stick. She returned to the nest to pluck out the soft matter that the squirrel had lined it with, and she put this soft matter into her boots for insulation, then what was left over she put into the sack for fire starting. She went back once more to discover a cache of nuts and saw in delight that they were good sweet filberts. Thank you, squirrel, she said to the furious thing that was now barking at her, perhaps in grief. She thought it wanted to leap upon her and bite her to death; its fury was justified, but it did not have the courage to come near.

Then, even within this mother squirrel's sight, feeling deeply indecent but, she thought in shame, she was so very hungry, she took more of the downy matter from the nest and some dry innards of bark and made a fire and roasted the baby squirrels, which were so tender that their bones melted as she chewed them. And because there was still some fire left, she dug out the fish's tail from the sack, as it had begun to stink, and broiled it upon the coals. Crouching, she finished it off and felt much better indeed. She had put her cup beneath a persistent drip from a branch, and by the time she had finished eating, she had caught enough melted snow to slake her thirst.

Now the mist thinned and the outlines of the trees in the near edge of the forest emerged, then even the trees in the distance came clear to her eye, if vague at their borders. The air was full of shining drops. When one without warning fell upon her head, it was so sudden and so cold that she had a thrill of indignation, as though someone had thrown an egg at her.

She walked as fast as she could while the earth was still hard and the mud had not yet thickened. In the melting, her passage would be slippery and slow, and she would get chilled in her wetted clothing, which, if she did not find fire soon enough, could mean a death of exposure.

To amuse herself as she walked, she began to imagine what form her savior might take, for she was raised to expect a savior, had been told from the moment of her birth that a savior would come to deliver her. She must be patient and humble herself for his arrival. This, too, was writ deep in her.

After thinking it through, and perhaps because the loss of the dutchboy was still in her heart, she felt sure that she would be delivered by a foreigner, a frenchman. For, she reasoned, though she had gone on foot over these nights, she had already traveled as far northward as most of the men of the fort who had gone in boats on their explorations, meeting the powhatan and pamunkey, and trading metal goods and linens and sugar for heaps of corn and dried fish. When they returned, these men were treated by the starving english with gratitude and the courtesy of diplomats, were listened to with credulous ears as they told stories of their meetings. So there would be no more people of her own country this far northward for many leagues, not until they haunted the frigid cod waters in the farthest north, and she could not work out how she would make them find her in all the spooling coastline. She would surely be too insignificant upon the shore to strike their eyes from where they fished, and even if she were to spend weeks constructing a bonfire large enough, surely it would draw the people native to the place instead of the english. And she did not think it possible she would survive being saved by the native people of the place, for surely she would die if she were among people who scorned and hated her god.

No, she thought of the frenchmen because she liked frenchmen mightily, because there were frenchmen among the lords and artists and writers who came to drink small beer in the mistress's house and eat her cakes. All of her beloved frenchmen had worn perfume in such quantities that it made her head swoon; it made her feel attacked gently by flowers. The best had been a man with a big red bloom of a nose and gout in his feet that made him take tiny steps, hissing like a gander, but with merriment in his eyes. He had liked the girl and had called her his toothsome morsel in his strange lisping accent, and pulled her into his lap, and, when the mistress was otherwise occupied, put his hand down her bodice, always leaving sweets there, candied lemon peels or ginger and sugared dates. Week after week he came to the mistress's afternoons, and each week he taught the girl a phrase in his language for a kiss. Zhemmlay-frahnsay, a kiss. Tooshay-mwah-laba, a kiss. For she had been trained up since four years of age to be a singing dancing mimicking parrot, and like this, with the kisses she did not so much care for but with the sweets she did, she had picked up enough french to converse with some pains.

Then she remembered the coarseness and need of this uncivilized country she had found herself within and laughed at herself, because no frenchman as fine as those who wore perfume and silken hose and powder upon their faces and rouge upon their cheeks would discover himself in such a place. No, the only ones to bring themselves here would be as rough as the men in the settlement she had fled from, or earthy farmers and soldiers and hunters, or the avid amoral sons of nobility who would murder to find themselves masters of more land and fortune than their eldest brothers.

It was for this reason, the girl suspected, that the minister, the mistress's second husband, had joined the company upon the ships. But because he was a hypocrite in his heart, as she knew well by then, his sermon one Sunday did paint a different story, a far more godly one. For there he had stood in the winter gleam through the church's windows and raised in the congregation's minds fiery visions of the poor benighted souls who lived in darkness on the distant continent, who lived ignorant of the love and mercy of the one true god. But though they were people of a godless continent, they, too, had been made in the mold of Adam; they, like the english, wore upon their bodies the likeness of the great creator. And it was the duty, nay!, the vocation, of all the holy englishmen of courage and true belief to go to where the most need was, to lift those souls caught in the darkness of ignorance upward to the light.

He gave a powerful pause and brought his hands together and cast upon all the congregation his most soulful, most beautiful look, then he announced that he had taken a place upon the next ship to the new world. And the hearts in the congregation had been stirred to joy by this news, and the collection plate was very heavy at the end of the day; and if some among the congregation were sorrowful for losing such a beautiful and silken-tongued minister as this one, for it was not only the women of the church who dreamed at night of him, they donated all the more heavily for their personal selfish pang of grief.

Only the girl had seen how the mistress, who had not known of this hasty decision made by her new husband, her second husband, drove her nails so deep into her own palms that they drew crescents of blood, and the girl had had to slip her own handkerchief between the mistress's bleeding hands and the fine pink stuff of her skirt to keep the blood off her dress.

At home, the mistress ordered all the maids to beat the rugs in the courtyard and the cook to sing at the fearsome top of her voice so that the neighbors would not hear the quarrel that she was squaring herself to begin. The girl helped the mistress off with her cloak and lingered only long enough to hear the mistress say in a tone full of daggers, The gift of god that you spoke of, my husband, is surely not the gift of faith you would so gently bestow upon the godless men of the new world, but rather the wealth and land that god would see fit to bless you with there, no?

Upon the minister's fine face there was a smile meant to soothe when he said, dulcet, Admit, my wife, that, with your esprit and beauty and music and taste, you would make a far finer duchess than that slut my brother's wife.

Verily, she said, but was not appeased and a moment later said, But I should rather be a minister's wife, even a minister's widow, than a one-month duchess of worthless distant lands, slain dead by an arrow in the throat.

To which he said, Aye, I have foreseen this, and I have made plans to leave you in england until I have been made comfortable in the new world, at which time I can send for you to receive you in the style to which you are accustomed.

And this, the girl knew, would be the true beginning of the fight, for the mistress was a jealous wife and saw threats to her marriage on all sides, as the girl thought she likely should, and would never countenance being left behind, for fear of the younger more beautiful women he would meet elsewhere. The girl crept out and went down the stairs. And in the kitchen, she tried not to listen but could not avoid hearing without stopping her ears with her fingers. As she listened, she felt her heart sink, for she knew that the body of the minister, the mistress's new husband, was a potent wine, and that it had made the mistress drunk with lust, and that there could be no parting her from her chosen drink. In this, the girl was proved right. The house was sold, the family furniture put into storage, the mistress's bad son Kit, new out of university, was given a cheaper house of his own with only three servants; and the mistress, the child Bess, and the girl were bought places upon the same ship as the minister. No one had thought to ask the girl if she had any wish to go. Only now did she understand that she, too, had not asked herself this question.

To rid herself of the bitter tang of the thought, she bent her mind again to the idea of her future savior. She walked, and in her thoughts, she built him up, making the place where he lived far to the north in the deep snow that she did not care about as long as she had a fire to warm herself beside. She set his cabin on a gleaming lake within green hills, then created his person, giving him the glassblower's wide innocent eyes in their rays of good humor, his own sweet face but perhaps under an uncut beard, the same height and large shoulders and hands with their gentleness and pink healed burns all over them. Her imaginings made the breath go out of her, and she could not look away from the bunchings of the muscles on her frenchman's back, which was also the back of her dutchboy.

She spent some time then building up the cabin, which would be close and dark to keep out the cold, but clean, with the corners heaped with soft pelts of mink and beaver that she and her trapper would make their bed in. They would keep smoked meat in the space dug into the earth beneath the floorboards, and all they would have to do was to open the trap and reach a knife in to cut off a goodly amount of venison or a dangling trout. Upon the shelves, she imagined cones of sugar so large that it would be impossible that they could be eaten in a lifetime, and good teas and herbs, and pepper and salt, and jars of jam and honey and dried fruits and nuts and flour. He would keep there some tobacco he would let her smoke in her own pipe, perhaps even a pipe made of clay in the face of a laughing man, like the friend of her dutchman had

had. One would not grow tired of the other because he would go out on his traplines during the passable weather, even deep into the spring, and she would wait in generous solitude in the warmth and cleanliness, and make a fine stew for him when he returned, and with the music she would sing in her loudest voice, she would scare off the coyotes and wolves that would skulk near to dig at the foundations to get at the meat inside. Some nights, alone, she would hear the same wolves singing in the hills and would not feel frightened, for inside the cabin, and with the trapper moving swift through the snow on his way back to her, she would be safe.

She decided she would like this quiet life with her good trapper, alone with him, naked with him in the open air, in the cabin lined with furs, at least for a few years. A woman at the fort had taught her a brew with an herb easily found in this place that was strong enough to avoid a babe planting itself in her womb, and she would drink it often, for giving birth with no woman nearby in the desolate wilderness would be unimaginable horror.

Then after he had furred so well that there was nothing more they could do, he would take the boat he had built with his two strong hands and sail up the river to the french fort, where he would exchange the furs for gold. They would cross the ocean again and this she did not yearn for; it gave her the goosebumps to imagine the crossing back, but it would be worth it when they climbed down from the ship in france to see all the beautiful dresses, smell the perfumes, eat the fine foods of a civilized city once more. Then they would go, quite wealthy now, able to afford a carriage, to his family's farm somewhere nice with cows. She had no real understanding of the geography of france, or the countryside for that matter; she was a girl who knew only the city and these desolate wastes. On the farm she would embrace his mother with all the beautiful language she had learned from him in their years of solitude and nature, and they would live happily upon the farm with many servants, buying all the adjoining farms, their wealth from the new world translated into pieces of the old. And all that would be asked of her, as a wife, would be to supervise the servants and taste the butter the dairy maids churned and grow old and quite fat with the good food she would not cease eating for a moment; she would eat until she could eat no more every day, for in this place she had known such depths of want. Yes, in her dotage she would grow enormous, so huge she would shake the floorboards when she walked, and she would taste all day the cheese and jams she made herself; she would have a life of good godly hard work and the love of her husband and would die of old age in a fine featherbed of her own, surrounded by kin who grieved the loss of her. She would not mind being a papist, even, and praying to a crucifix, and believing in saints. For, despite the horror in which papists were held in her country, she was quietly sure that though the trappings differed, still the god of the papists was the very same god to all christians. And the deaths of all the people who have insisted otherwise were tragedies that need not happen. But of course men, particularly the godly ones, have little common sense.

Buoyed these many miles by her daydreams of her future, she walked the entire morning through.

She had become so sunk in her imaginings that she lost sight of her direction.

Midmorning, she looked down and saw a bootprint in the mud. She stopped.

A boot means a foot, she thought.

A booted foot means a christian man.

A booted foot this far north, this far from the french, means a man of her people is following her, that she is being hunted like an animal.

Her heart seized in her chest and she felt such terror that she crouched where she was and made a noise, then hated herself for making the noise.

Crouched here, with her cloak with the hood pulled over her face and her hands covered by the leather gloves, perhaps she would not be visible as a human form; perhaps she would blend with the small brown tussocks in the woods.

But up close she saw even through her terror the small size of the bootprint in the mud, which was her own size. And when she looked up, she saw the same meadow she had passed through some hours earlier but in her dreamings had not fully marked before. And that wispy and leaning pine tree at the edge she had certainly seen, for, suffused by affection for her imaginary life, she had given its trunk a loving pat as she walked past it.

She had been walking in circles, she understood at last. She pressed her knuckles to her eyes and breathed deep to calm herself and chase away the white-hot anger at herself that had risen in place of the fear.

In time, she remembered a little boy in the fort who had showed her a trick. Like the boy, she broke off a long stick and pushed it into the ground and marked the end of the stick's shadow with a stone. She drank water as she waited, and pissed and ate the last of the filberts she had stolen from the poor squirrel.

When the shadow had moved, she marked the new end of the shadow and thus was able to draw a line from west to east, and thus she understood where north was to be discovered. Then in that direction she sighted the line of a near tree, then a farther tree, then a third and farthest tree, and keeping them in a row in her sight, she moved on.

Much later, as the afternoon waned, she came upon a stretch of forest so recently burnt that it was as though she were walking through a land leached of all color; all was black and gray, and there was no sound at all of bird or beast alive here. She thought of her night terror, the gray and black landscape and the great beasts of bone rising to walk through it, the plaques of dried earth falling from their joints, and trembled. She would not linger in this place. The papists believed, she had heard, in a place called purgatory where souls go to wait; and purgatory was not heaven, not hell, but rather a third, indeterminate place, where babes, who were not evil, for babes had not yet developed the organs of evil, but who were unbaptized, stumbled about, and the noblest souls among the heathens played shuttlecock with the ghosts of doves. The spirits of animals went there, she had heard; the land was thick with the souls of the slaughtered. This seemed to her akin to the place she had walked into, this burnt forest.

Then, below the scorched skeleton of an enormous oak, she found an abundance of fire-dried mushrooms that she sat to taste. How good they were, smoky and rich. She waited for the poison to begin to swell her tongue or the wild dreams to commence—servants in the fort were always plucking a certain wild mushroom that they ate to give themselves colorful dreams that made the misery in life bearable—but after some time and feeling no ill effect, she pronounced the mushrooms good. She picked every one she could find and stowed them in her sack.

Then she walked her way through the last light back into the un-burnt world, where the still-bare bushes glowed with good health, where the birds sang and argued overhead, where she could nearly hear the sap rising fresh in whispering song within the living trees.

At the top of a rise, she came into a clearing and saw in her astonishment a tangle of blackberry bushes so thick and so tall that even the smallest and nimblest of birds and the thickest-pelted bears could not have stripped the winter-dried berries away no matter how fully they ate. The beasts and birds had touched only the external berries and there were plenty of dried berries still remaining within the bushes. If she inserted her arms carefully into the thorny tangles and cut with the knife until her body could pass within the opening, she could reach the dried berries and pluck them into her sack. But first she filled her mouth, and tears came into her eyes with the sharpness of the berries, then the sweet.

She put berries into the sack, then into her mouth again, and alternated between the two until she had nearly more than she could carry; the sack bulged. She felt sick again in her stomach and had to remove herself delicately from the tangles and squat beside a tree and let out in a delicious flood the foul loose shit that the berries and the mushrooms before them had stirred out of her guts. She drank down the water from the slow drip off a tree that she'd had the foresight to set the pewter cup under.

By now, the twilight had begun to thicken, however; and she had to find some shelter before thick night came on full of its roving predators. She sensed that it would be a very cold night as well.

When she stood, she found she had a hard time moving swiftly; she was so stiff and sore from her long walk.

The ground, in the warming day, had become tricky. The path she was following, if it was indeed a path, was now overwhelmed with streams that poured down from the melting, and in places she had to pick her way very carefully across churning water and mud that slopped and sucked at her boots.

By the time she could not see very far ahead, she had found nothing to cover her, and she had begun to worry.

And this was when she saw a little black space carved out of the rock wall of a ridge that rose to the height of a roof's peak into the sky beside her. She came close and the dark mouth of the cave exhaled a strange and musty warmth that drew her near.

Something in her said to her that she must be cautious, and she made herself go slowly and silently. But soon the coldness of the night oncoming frightened her more than the cave with all its menacing unknowns. She ducked low into the black space and felt instantly that it would be warm enough and out of the melting wet at least. It smelled dank and thick in there. The darkness welled and seemed to pulse at the back of the cave.

She hurried back out and spent the last of her forces gathering up in her arms some dry wood for the fire, searching for pockets of unsoaked matter to use as kindling. Then she took her hatchet and cut some soft and living branches from the fir trees to make a mattress for her body against the cold stone floor, which would steal the warmth down out of her flesh and replace it with cold. The branches smelled so clean and pungent that she had a hope they might drive away from her the vermin that bedeviled her scalp and groin and pits, and caused her a low and constant irritation.

Now, knowing the comfort of sleep was awaiting her inside the cave, she got a small fire going and watched as the night poured full over the trees in the little valley she had passed through. And far away, the final cold flare of sun uplit in red the sharp spines of trees along a distant rise. Then all the light suddenly went out, and the moon rose into its seat in the deep dark blue sky.

In the firelight, she took all of her good things out of her sack to care for them, because they were the only friends she had and they each had begun to grow some character. The hatchet was blunt but as faithful as a dog, the knife was two-faced and angry but always ready, the flint was taciturn, the sack bemused, the coverlets pacific, the pewter cup over-eager and a little greedy. Off her feet she took the twin boots, her best two friends and the most doughty, even though the left boot had a nail working its way up from under the sole, and the nail worried her mightily. She picked the clinging seeds and sticks and mud off her cloak, and dug the boots out of their thick coating of filth, then she polished them with the hem of an interior gown until in the small light they gleamed.

Having staved off her hunger for as long as she felt willing, she took two handfuls of the dried berries and some mushrooms, and ate them together, which was a lovely taste, at the same time rich and tart and sweet and smoky. Then she lay down to sleep, having made her fire a little too hot and large because the malevolent darkness at the back of the cave still felt wrong to her, as though it were a single large dark watchful eye. And though she felt her body yearning for sleep, her imagination sparked in a hundred directions, wondering what that blackness might contain. She was a fool, she knew, even as she populated the cave with beast and man. But she couldn't stop her imaginings. They filled her with pulses of fear.

She tried to calm herself by listening to her blood in her ears and was terrified when, as she watched the fire flickering on the stone above, a sudden black eruption of bats squealed by in a swift tarry stream and disappeared out of the mouth of the cave into the trees. Her heart thudded, but the bats did not return.

Slowly the vigilance in her seeped out. Sleep seeped in.

In the depths of the night, when the fire had burned itself to embers, she startled awake with premonition.

She knew to keep her eyes squeezed shut, hold her breath, and keep her limbs stiff to pretend that her body was dead.

For she had sensed, and now she heard, its large shufflings nearing her, its hot breaths at her feet and knees, her groin, her neck, her head. In her nostrils, though she dared not breathe, there rose a sickening odor of animal body and rot and mildew and something deeper, a musk, so thick that though she was not breathing she could taste it on her tongue.

And she imagined a jagged wet mouth opening on her head, the grip of the teeth, the squeeze then the pop of her skull, and the slick slide into death. She imagined talons, the rasping of scales, the folded wrinkled enormous bat wings of a dragon.

But whatever beast this might have been gave a low moan that made her body bloom in cold goosebumps, then it slid its weight to the other side of the fire, farther beyond her, then out beyond the mouth of the cave. She could hear it plodding with its heavy footsteps through the trees into the night; she listened until she could hear it no more.

And only then she allowed herself to breathe, for death had been a hair from her. She fought to open her eyes for fear of what she would see. But it was dark in the cave, so dark that she could barely see her metal things gleaming where she had placed them around herself, and she gathered them up with fast hands and shoved the two coverlets into the sack as well and laced her boots back on and fled as fast as she could move up the path away from the lair of what she had envisioned as a dragon, a great snakeskinned black thing with a lumbering tail, a strange beast of these strange lands.

Strangest of all was the beast's whim to extend mercy to a mouthful like her, the girl thought.

Surely this mercy would be fleeting and the beast would return at a run to repent.

She ran faster away.

She flew as fast as she could over the mud thinly frozen again in the chill night, into the wild dark woods, because what was behind her was far more deadly than whatever could lie ahead.

And in the sky, the swift black clouds frighted the fixed stars and made them tremble.

At a distance from the cave, a league or so perhaps, she allowed herself to stop and breathe until the pain in her lungs dissolved. She was too hot, she was sweating, and she needed to act quickly, as her body was wet now and was cooling, and she knew that such cold wetness could make her ill with the freezing wind if she did not act against it.

Though she was weary, she forced herself to go on in order to stay warm and try to dry her clothing with her body's heat. The wind was harsh in the night. Every step made her wince. Only when her body had cooled enough to make her hands cold, and she searched for her leather gloves, did she discover that she had left them in the cave, where she had taken them off to care for her things. She could now see them in the evening fire's gleam, set absurdly in prayer position near the fire to dry.

And this was like a physical blow to her chest, for now her hands would be naked and exposed to the elements, to cuts and scrapes. She had to hold her head to the clean bark of a chestnut tree and breathe there for some time to let her sorrow pass.

7.

On she pressed through the night. She sang the songs of her dancing-fool youth until she had come to the end of her memory and did not want to sing them all through again, then she counted her footsteps but this did not take long for she did not know in truth what came after nine hundred ninety-nine though she understood vaguely that at some point a thousand came in. What education she had was accidental, the gleanings of talk that she had absorbed by chance and the pictures in the books that the mistress's boy Kit had showed her either to display his superior understanding or to frighten her.

Deep in the night, she saw an opening in the path and came out into a broad dim plain. It was, she understood, the second river to the north of the settlement, and the ice over the water had broken up in the thaw of the last days. The floes struggled against each other, moaning and squealing, bringing to her mind a great pen of pigs. She knew when looking at them that there would be no crossing here by foot. She saw herself leaping, a flea, from floe to floe and laughed because she would soon slip and fall in and drown. But then she stopped laughing and wept.

For some time, she allowed herself the luxury of despair, crouching with her head cradled by her arms. When she stood again and wiped her face, she knew that there was nothing to do but move upstream, to the west, away from the bay to the east, and she would follow this bank of the river until she could find a fording place where the river became thin and shallow enough to cross.

Soon her eye fell on a black mass in the reeds at the edge of the river, and she bent to stare at two ducks curled together, sleeping with necks folded, in their new-built nest. A bounty, a gift, she thanked god for it silently. She reached beneath the body of the female duck, which was too tired from her exertions to sense the girl, and felt the good eggs there, laid mere hours earlier. There were three, and the girl took them one by one into her sack. Then she considered the two ducks, knowing that she couldn't carry both and maintain her speed. She selected the female with a sorrowful heart, for the female duck was smaller and exhausted by her labors.

The girl took the duck by the head and lifted it and swung it and broke the neck so quickly that the male did not even sense in his slumber that his mate was gone.

In the morning, he would awaken to find his dream of mate and nest and ducklings had been robbed of him in the night; he would find himself lonely, and he would wail with the sound of a trumpet and flap his wings and burst up into the sky because his grief could find no other outlet than in flying.

She felt a pang in imagining this, for she herself had known the confused search for one now gone.

By then, however, the girl would be far away, in a tight ring of fir trees blocking the wind, having made a little tent of a coverlet to smoke the meat of the female duck and roast its eggs in the embers of the fire so as to save them for a bit longer. She would collect the dripping duck fat in her cup until it congealed, then she would dump it into a little basket that she had woven of dried reeds while waiting for the cooking to finish, and she would attach the clever basket to her waist by a strip of torn hem so that the fat would stay cool and solid in the broad air. And this fat she would spread upon her hands, which, without the gloves even in these few hours since she had lost them, had chapped and were bleeding in places, and thus she would find small relief there. But still in the deep of the night and carrying the burden of the dead duck and her fragile eggs, the girl moved up the bank cautiously. Her body was too tired by now to allow her any deeper thought.

When the dawn at last rose on a flat white day, she had fallen into a sleep so deep that she was unaware of the first birdsong that shifted the whole of the world into action.

In her sleep, a voice spoke to her. What, girl, is the purpose of your journey? the voice said.

I want to live, the girl said. If I stop I will die.

You are willing, the voice said, to suffer so greatly?

I have known suffering before, she said.

Not so great as this, the voice said.

I am not the first to suffer, for Job endured worse and was rewarded for bearing in humility the tests of god, she said.

What if your sufferings are not the tests of god but rather punishments for your acts, for your corrupted soul? the voice said.

Then, the girl said angrily in her sleep, I shall bear the suffering in gratitude for the life that has already been granted me, and because I have repented my sins, I know that I would be saved in eternity.

And though she said this, still something in her stirred uneasily. She pushed it behind the door in her mind with a sense of strain. It was her true culpability, her hands remembering the wet hot slick in the night.

She woke feeling within her a glimmer of unfairness, for she knew very well that there were far worse souls than hers in the world, evil ones who were even now delighting in the taste of hot codlings and beautiful wines on the tongue. Who were having their faces powdered and silks settled upon their bodies and perfumes applied heady on their necks and wrists.

Even the cook with her fine blond beard, who was one of the worst of all people back at home in the city, had not been forced to come to this wild place. She had been a shrewish nasty sharp-tongued woman who hit the littlest maids with her long iron spoon so that welts came up on their buttocks and backs, and once she broke a fishmonger's wagon with three hard kicks because he had dared to bring her too-old sturgeon. And yet though a thoroughly bad person, a person who would never come near the gates of heaven when her soul departed her body, the cook had not been the one forced into this living death; she had not been forced to walk onto the boat that carried them across the ocean; she had not been brought to bear such terrible sufferings as even the innocent gentle child Bess had had to endure in the fort. Today, the cook would have woken to the music of churchbells of early morning in the new household that had taken her in, and would have started the fire all alone in the kitchen and put the bread in the communal oven to bake, and in time, she would have had hot brown bread and small beer to break her fast; and beyond the doors of her household, there was stirring the great city full of its comforts and entertainments and food and delight and other souls who perhaps loved even such a bitter sharp-ish woman as she.

But it is I, who had lived only to love, to serve, who finds herself alone in this place, the girl thought.

And I am poor and needy, and my heart is wounded within me; I am gone like the shadow when it declineth; I am tossed up and down like the locust; my knees are weak through fasting and my flesh faileth of fatness.

Then the girl let her bitterness pass, and said, All my life I have done my duty, I have done my best, and in my self I know that I have sinned, and I accept these sufferings in my own penitence.

Still, the dark of her fault remained, a shadow within her.

The knife again so furious in her hand, the slickness of the guts on the blade.

For god in his wrath was just.

She felt swallow her acceptance of her transgressions, a settling within. Then she rose and cast the sorrow behind her and set her sight forward on what she must do to stay alive.

But now, with the ground in its melting all damp and muddy and the edge of the river vague with marshlands full of reeds and filth to the knees, her passage up the grain of the river was far more difficult.

She struggled and the cold mud seeped into her boots and made each step unpleasant.

The afternoon was warmer even than the previous, and she saw no more white in the world save for the broken ice in the river and one slight cloud etched above in the blue.

When she looked hard, she could even see a hint of green upon the branches, and when she stopped, she was overjoyed to discover that they were buds at the ends of the bolder kinds of trees. She nibbled at them and was pleased to find some tender and peppery. She could make a meal of these.

I give thanks, o my lord, to find that this stark wasteland in which I wander is far less hostile than I had so deeply feared, she thought.

And as she went along, she plucked and ate the soft new leaves, and she walked with the fresh green taste upon her tongue.

8.

At midday, she stopped and ate one of the roasted duck eggs and drank the breathtaking cold river water. She dried her boots and the three pairs of stockings at the fire she built, first warming a stone at the edge of it so to rest her feet in comfort while she waited.

She washed and examined her feet, which were doing rather poorly. They were monstrous sore and swollen and pink, and the heels were raw, having grown blisters that popped and bled and grew more blisters in the deeper, more tender flesh beneath.

Far worse, she saw, was that the nail working up through the sole of the left boot had begun to carve a bloody trench out of the bottom of her foot. She hit at the nail with the handle of the hatchet until she had beat it somewhat down again, and with the knife, she carefully cut a doubled thickness of the woolen coverlet to insert into the bottom of the boot.

When she was finished with her labors, the fire's heat had dried the blisters somewhat, and the skin over the wounds had tightened. The open wound on the bottom of her heel had stopped bleeding and had begun to pulse. She packed one stocking further with some dry vegetable fluff gathered from last year's reeds, then held it in place by wrapping the torn hem of her bottom gown around it, over and over. This way, she thought, if the nail wanted to bite her when she walked, it would bite only fabric, not skin.

Although she had believed it safe to have a little fire to dry and warm her, it was unwise. She could not have known how very unwise it was.

For the smoke had drawn new notice. A man had come creeping to see the source of the disturbance in the air. And now he sat in wonderment, watching within the shadows of the forest; and deep within him, a monstrous tumult moved.

He was not a man original to this place. This would have been clear to the girl if she had been able to see him, but what he was would have been mightily difficult for her to fathom. He seemed a chimera, half man, half beast. Human eyes were embedded within a matted mass of hair from the scalp, which had grown all together into the hair from the beard and the back and the shoulders and chest so that he wore a filthy seedy twiggy tunic out of which lower arms and legs did poke. His hair-tunic was black at the edges but yellowed by sun and years, fully grayed in the most recent hair, where it grew out of the mouth and temples. And what was not covered by the hair-tunic was covered by a motley rug of the hides of small game, chipmunk and muskrat and squirrel and hare, pieced together with dried gut. At the ends of the hands, his nails curled in talons of yellow horn. And on the feet, two male coneys had been skinned whole for shoes and were tied upon the ankles by the long ears. He smelled like something long dead.

Forty years earlier, this man had been a spanish jesuit priest who had come up the river to the south on a boat to form a mission there. He had been young then, quick and witty and laughing, a handsome curly-haired boy. He spent the long voyage out from spain learning some of the powhatan tongue from the guide, a boy who had been captured on a previous mission and taken to la florida and taught the language and religion of the spanish. The guide liked him, and in return for the pow-hatan language, the guide learned latin from the young spaniard. For, as the priest had been given to the jesuits as a babe barely walking, he spoke latin with an ease and delight equal to the spanish he had first learned from his mother, who gave him away. But the jesuits in their disregard angered the men who received them on their land, and after a summer of the missionaries' putting up their dormitory building and their church with its iron bell, and planting what vegetables they could plant into the ground, they had a long hungry winter during which they bartered away all their metal goods one by one for food. They became—it seemed impossible—yet more demanding of their hosts, not asking for help but shrilly insisting upon it. As well, they told the people of this place that if they did not kneel to the water-walking three-headed god of the spanish, they would remain heathens and thus burn after death in a place of long torture. And this, the powhatan felt, was a terrible unkind thing for these uninvited guests of their hospital-ity to insist upon. And so they planned to move against the priests one night. And the boy guide, who had been returned to his own people but did love the young priest, asked the other to go for a long walk with him during the night the raid was planned. And the young priest who trusted his friend walked with him in the fresh cold moonlight and together talked of many things, of god and love and hunger and the way that, the priest believed at that time, beauty washed the soul of the befoulments of sin. By the time they turned back, the mission was on fire and all the priests lay dead in their cots within with their necks slit open and the blood of their hearts rushing to the ground.

Then the guide in his pity and love raised his club toward his friend and made a threatening face, and the other saw murder there; he had seen the glow of the burning mission upon the horizon, and he ran off in terror into the woods with nothing more to help him but what he bore upon his body.

He stumbled about for weeks, nearly starving in that time, and a deep madness set in, but the powhatan who were watching him from a distance put nuts and fresh game in his way, and he survived. At last, he discovered the hollow of a giant oak tree, which he dug out further with the iron cross around his neck and oyster shells until it became a cave as large inside as one of the stone shepherd's huts in the fields of his native alicante. And this tree hovel he made safe and tight against the elements with mats woven of reeds, and he decorated it inside with shelves made of branches and stones, upon which he put the nuts and berries and wild rice and dried fish and knobby tuber ends of cattails and other bits of vegetables that became food if they did not poison him. In time, he taught himself to fish by building weirs in the shallows of stone, how to trap small beasts with snares of grapevine and sinew and stick and stone. He slept deep from twilight to dawn, and in this way, without any knife or fire to keep him warm in the depths of winter and cook his meat, he lived for nearly forty years. The meat he ate was raw. All this time he was full of worms.

He did not know that his countrymen had landed again not so very far from where he was and, in vengeance for the massacred priests, had painted the earth red with the blood of the natives, women and children and old men, and set fire to their buildings, and sailed off home again, for empire has no pity and is never sated.

While he lived alone in his stock of a tree, he spoke to himself in a latin that in time lost all of its declensions and tenses and moods and participles and, like his sanity, became a fabric of tatters and holes.

He began to believe of himself that he was a holy hermit, that he had been directed to the wilderness by the invisible hand of god and held there to do the work of god. He called himself Sanctus Ioannes Cavae Arboris. The powhatan, who had never forgotten this strange man in the woods, who often left him a surplus of food in the occasional form of fresh deer in his path and creatures they put in his snares and heaps of nuts where he would find them, which he believed to be entirely the fruit of his own cleverness, thought of him as a benign demon of the trees, and one not without powers, for he had survived these many years in a density of solitude. And humans were not made to be always alone; humans survive only in the company of other humans.

All this time, his only interlocutors had been the crows, the many descendants from a nest of chicks he'd stolen one lonely spring and raised by hand and taught to speak in nearly human utterances. He fed them the bones and entrails of his prey, and communicated with them in strange barking noises, and they, in turn, became his flying eyes and told him when he had snared his prey, warned him when the weather was about to turn, played small games of toss with him using a walnut or a round white stone. It was the crows who had alerted their man to the smoke down at the riverbank, to the creature unknown to them, a strange beast not like the other human beasts of the place.

Now he crouched, hidden and breathless, watching a person there in the woven clothing of christians, which he had not seen in the entirety of his hermitage. He longed to hold the cloak of wool in his hand, to press the softness to his face and smell the good lanolin of the sheep within its weave, for he had loved the sheep his birth parents had raised, their stupid faces and their hopeful bleatings and their sweet gamboling joyous lambs in the spring. It had been many lifetimes since he had held the makings of other human hands in his own.

And this particular form of human, the kind with breasts, he had seen only a handful of occasions in his long years in the woods, but they were of the native peoples of this place, moving on the river in the silent distant boats they had paddled there, and he was never close enough to touch the flesh of one.

And the fire, too, he gazed upon hungrily, for he had not known fire for so long, had learned to live without it though there had been times he thought verily he would die of the cold. In about four decades, as he cleaved to the same paths in a short radius around his tree-hovel, he had only ever seen the distant smoke of the powhatan a few times and the fire of lightning in the skies. Now he was smelling smoke and it stirred in him a gladness, a sweet tender sorrowful gladness; and he thought of the chambers of his kind jesuit master who brought him up and taught him, the hearth in his bedroom and the rug beautifully plush and patterned and from the orient upon which the master often allowed the boy to fall asleep curled up for special comfort.

Now he looked upon this tiny person in the filthy woven clothing and her flint and her hatchet and her knife, and thought perhaps this meant that there were other christians in the vicinity. But he knew there could not be. For he had seen no upwellings of black smoke that christian men use to clear the land of trees, which they certainly would do if there were even a small settlement nearby. For if god's own best-beloved jesuits could be driven from this place in massacre, could be taught that this was no place for them, then certainly no other christians could possibly be godly enough for the powhatan to allow them to set a single foot upon this land.

He muttered aloud in a low voice, in his tattered latin, that this before him was a thing he must be careful about.

This was a thing, a thing; he had lost the name of such things as these, that bleed out of the place of shames. Things of breasts, of holes. Bad things, Eve things, harlot things, mother things, wife things, baby-making things. She things. These not-men things. O it would not return, the name of this kind of human. These things that had been flushed with evil since the wife of Adam was bitten by the snake that made her eat the fruit and thus condemn all mankind to inherent sin. For surely, if there were no christians nearby and of course there were not, this she-thing could not be really here.

Surely, this she-thing was a devil sent by god to torment him again.

For devils over the long years had come in all forms to him, all kinds of monstrous forms, as small as mosquitoes pricking and pricking his uncovered nose, and when he smashed them with his hand, he saw the smashed mosquitoes were no mosquitoes but ruddy devils with cloven hooves and fangs and three-pronged tails. Far more malignant devils had often come to him also, to goad and taunt him, squirrel bodies with the faces of tiny wizened men, and wild boars that had a ridge of glorious white plumes along their backs and red lights in their eyes, and demons dragging long wet fish tails behind their scurrying tortoise feet and exhaling breath that smelled like all the sulfur released from hell. There had been far too many demons over the years that he had had to fight and vanquish in murdering. Each he had wrestled with until he panted and was exhausted, until, in the end, he had slain them and, in killing, proved the strength of his devotion to his ever-testing god.

Now he looked upon this not-man warming those purple toes upon the fire and cleaning her boots, which he longed for, with what he first saw as a stick, then with a gasp recognized as the cold glint of metal. A knife, yes, a knife, what he could do with a knife!

Pater noster qui es in caelis, santificetur nomen tuum. Adveniat regnum tuum. Fiat voluntas tua, sicut in caelo et in terra. Cultrum nostrum quotidianum da nobis hodie.

He knew now truly that this creature, too, was a demon come to tempt him.

And that he must slay this thing also to prove again his faith.

And so from the ground he plucked up two stones perfect for throwing.

But he did not throw, not yet, for it was no sin, surely, to wait. To enjoy the sight of this not-man. It had been so long since he had seen one, and it was also true that when he was a youth, though promised from wordless infancy to the jesuits and nearly always scrupulously holy in his waking thoughts, he would often dream in his sleep of the shameful parts of these not-men, their giant fleshy breasts and the soft damp holes he had been told in a whisper by another oblate that they wore in place of their members, where the male members were meant to bury themselves. He would waken from such dreams troubled and with a wetness in his clothing. And also true, he did find such creatures pleasing to the eye and, O he repented! it must be said, once or twice pleasing to the touch, having been lured out with the other oblate into the sevilla night and having sobbed with repentance even as he lowered himself into the body of a whore. The long-slumbrous part of him began to stir.

Upon the bank, the not-man wrapped torn fabric around her foot and put back on the many stockings though some were as thin as lace, all holes, and muddied through; and she tied with her fingers the latchets on the boots, which seemed as stiff as wood, having dried. Then she ate a large egg, with the shell peeling off the pearly globe of it, marvelous; he had forgotten what fire could do to eggs. And she drank from a cup—a cup! he nearly wept to see it—and put all her things within a sack that she tied beneath her skirts. He saw a flash of her hairy shame between her legs, and he looked avidly to see more but there was no more to see.

Then the she-devil settled the woolen cloak upon her shoulders and stood in seeming pain and set off on the gravel and shale of the riverbank. So quick she was, this not-man, so nimble and sure, and though the man watching knew these woods as well as his own body, he still had trouble keeping up with her.

Just when he was fatigued enough to consider throwing the first stone and braining the demon, for it was wearisome to track a thing so exceeding swift over miles, she came to where he had stowed the boat he had carved with oyster shells from a downed tree. And moons and moons it had taken him, and daily sweating labor, and it was his dear love, this boat, which gave him the means to move after fish, to tend to his weirs and to pass long afternoons of peace in the summer sun, trailing his hand in the water and gazing at the beauty and turmoil down below in the deeps. The demon gave a whispered word of happiness, then kicked his boat and it made a sound like a struck drum. Then so fast that he did not understand what she was doing, she thrust off the branches that masked the boat and looked around with narrowed eyes and crouched, then took in her hands the piece of driftwood that had been polished by his own, perfect for paddling, and thrust the boat and herself within it smooth into the water.

There she levered the driftwood paddle against the stones of the shore until the boat was full out and moving with the current full of ice, for the current had gathered the boat up in its hand and thrown it into the river so fast that he was still frozen in astonishment when he understood that the demon was only just within the range of his throw.

Then he ran out of the woods bellowing with grief for all that he was now losing, his boat, the she-demon to wrestle with his body perhaps, and the good things she had hidden within the sack she had stowed under her skirts, the hatchet the cup the knife the coverlets the flint which meant fire.

She in the boat saw this wild creature coming out of the forest squalling, a not-man not-beast, a monster from her night terrors sparked into full day, and she screamed and paddled wildly with the driftwood paddle, pushing hard off the chunks of ice.

He waded knee-deep into the freezing water and threw the first stone, and it fell shy of the boat by inches.

But the second stone he threw with desperation, and it flew through the air, and it landed true.

It hit the girl on the hardest part of her skull, at the height of her crown.

She fell backward into the boat, and for a long sick breath, the man was sure it would tip the demon into the water and she would drown, but instead the boat steadied itself against a large block of ice.

Still she remained fallen and he thought with pride that she must certainly be dead, for nothing could survive such a blow to the head; he had killed many a doe and turkey and muskrat and fox with an equal strike.

But the current carried the boat away faster than he could keep up with it. The river was stealing the boat and the knife and the cup, all of such things, from him; it was stealing his boat.

He stood upon the bank weeping after it. He would have far fewer fish to eat, for he could not tend his deeper weirs now. Worse, he could not ascertain if he had killed the demon dead, and had no proof of his faith to show his god.

And his furs, they were wet all the way up to his own dangling shame, which curled frightened nearly inside his body.

And his crows in the trees were laughing at him, screaming with laughter, for they had the sort of dark humor that took pleasure in the agony of others. He shook his fist at the birds, he cursed them in hate, they burst off the tree into the sky.

Later, he coaxed the ember that the girl had left behind into the first fire he had known in decades. He would cook the meat of a beaver over it and would gasp to discover it a hundredfold tenderer to his palate than it would have been raw. But now he stopped blowing upon the ember and struck himself on the cheek.

It had come to him at last.

Femina, he said sadly out loud, the word, as with everything this fated day, arriving too late.

9.

Through the long afternoon, the boat rode the current, the bow having caught upon a floe that pushed it toward the bay.

Birds circling above in curiosity saw that inside the boat there was a human girl who was a palish blue hue, as though dead, and across her skull was spreading and blackening a contusion like a unicorn's horn growing under her skin. But when some of the birds dipped to taste her, they discovered that she was still alive, for her teeth clacked and scared the birds back into flight. The water that had seeped up through the cracks in the boat and licked under the girl's clothes and at her ear and cheek had chilled her body to unconscious shivering.

In her dream, she was on a beach where all was gray: sky, stones, ocean with its waves that did not constantly move and crash but were frozen, unmoving.

She looked around and could not understand, there was nothing here, it was water and stone. At last, far off, at the limits of her sight, she saw what she knew was the child Bess.

Now she was running over the stones toward her beloved girl, slipping falling hurting sliding trying to get to her. No matter what, she could not reach the girl Bess, and she began to weep inside her dream. Outside, her face in her sleep became wet with tears and sweat, which under the wind soon became a white rime upon her cheeks and eyelashes.

Her dream self arrived at the child Bess, as if she'd given a hop and gone a league in the air and landed just beside the child, who was sitting in a chair, her hands folded in her lap and her posture exquisite, as it never was in life, she who was as slovenly and playful as a kitten, spilling all manner of foodstuffs and filth upon her neat pretty dresses so that they had to cover her in an old petticoat of rough linen to keep her good garments clean. She was facing the stilled ocean. Her flaxen hair was loosed and the ends of it were blown by the wind, and they were so long that they licked at the stones below. And looking upon the hair, which the girl had brushed so often, even in the dream she cried out in sorrow because the child was the dearest thing she had ever beheld. She was as simple and blank as a mirror and, like a mirror, the reflection of what the viewer saw in herself. From the time the mistress knew of the child Bess's impediment, her mind that remained in infancy even though her body grew and ripened, the mistress saw in her daughter her own weakness as a woman, her own insufficiencies and bald inferiority to any man around her, and held a hard and self-gnawing shame for her daughter and did not like to find herself near the child. But the girl Lamentations, though a mere servant of the household, had always looked upon the face only a few years younger than her own and saw the courage that it took to carry herself through the day in all her frailty; she saw what godly obedience the child held in the silence of her mind and what touching eagerness to please she held in her heart.

And here in this place of frozen death, at least her hair flowed, living, in the wind.

But in the girl dreaming, there rose a horror, because she soon understood that if she were to walk around to the front of the child Bess's chair, she would find her best beloved's face erased, only a slick of perfect unmarked flesh where those gentle brown eyes and nose and pert little flower of a mouth had been.

And so she did not move around to look at the girl; she was so hungry to see her again but did not. She stood behind her and put her hands in the yellow silk of her hair, but it, instead of feeling like hair, felt cold, like tiny fine flexible icicles, and it made her cry out in sorrow.

She woke when the water that had been leaking into the boat deepened from her fingertips to her wrists and chilled the edges of her ears. When she grasped the gunwales and pulled herself up, her head ached so horrendously that she vomited in the river. The sack around her waist was half soaked in water, and the thirsty fabric pulled the water up its sides; and with pain and frozen fingers, she lifted her skirts and untied the sack from her waist and put it on her lap in the dryness. The afternoon was dimming, it would soon be twilight, she was shuddering with cold, her whole back was soaked through with frigid water, her toes unmoving in the boots. Ahead of her, she could see the mouth of the bay opening in the terrifying distance. Though she was near insensible with her wounded head, she could work out from the low sun which of the banks of the river was the northernmost one. She pushed the boat off the floe that had saved her, and the boat glided for a long moment deeper into the river before it reached another floe. And like so, pushing and paddling and wincing in the wind, the girl made her way through the ice to the other bank before night fell hard and black upon the river.

She thought with a pang that perhaps it was not far enough from the matted beast-man, for who knew what powers of speed and endurance he bore, who knew if there were other beasts like him or even far worse beasts belonging to this strange place. Yet between the certain death if her boat were to be drawn into the roaring atlantic or the possible death of unknown malevolencies, she chose the mere possible.

The wind was biting, and she wept aloud as she waded out toward land, pulling the boat up behind her with the end of her strength. She knew she had to take her wet clothing off and wrap herself in the single blanket that was mostly dry, but she wept louder to do it, to expose her sparse blue flesh to the wind, though once she was inside the blanket, she was warmer. She found driftwood close to hand and it was dry and she gathered it in her arms, but she was shaking so wildly and her hands were so cold that it took her a very long time to build her fire. She thought that surely she would perish before a spark ever caught. But, after some despair, it did. She built the fire as large as she could, for survival trumped not alerting the people and creatures of this place to her presence, and she laid out her many dresses in their separate drying spaces, and the wet coverlet before the fire, and moved them until they were scorched dry. There she huddled close to the fire, drawing the heat into her until her skin felt burned by it.

And then upon a flat rock, she put the berries and mushrooms that had grown wet and sticky and clumped together, and tried to dry the mess, for she could still eat it. She ate the last duck egg, which was soft, but could not manage chewing the duck flesh, for harder chewing set off sparks in the bones of her skull.

When she took up a burning brand out of the fire to find more dry wood for the night, she saw that all the pockets where the small rocks caught and held the river water shone upward, as though they were countless glowing eyes caught watching her move.

She felt the knot on her head with her fingers—the skin taut there and a pounding tenderness within so that the lightest touch made her vision swim—and, when she had the strength again, she took another burning brand from the fire and carried it to a little still pool and saw in the reflection her own face made monstrous. Her skin was stained purple from the contusion all down her face, her eyes spots of flashing feeling from deep within the spread of the bruise all around them. Her cheeks had sunk in her hunger until her teeth revealed themselves, the mouth stretched back as if she were snarling.

Once, strangers had cupped her chin and marveled at the delicacy of her features and her long curled eyelashes and the rose and brown of her complexion. She was delighted in for the way she had walked behind the mistress in the market with her own tiny basket, to all watchers the very replica of the mistress before her, and the women selling their foodstuffs laughing with pleasure to see them, the tall powdered dazzling woman in her finery and the miniature same behind. They slipped the girl little pieces of fruit and slivers of cheese as one feeds treats to a pet dog. And even the dry antique goldsmith, the mistress's first husband and father of bad Kit and the child Bess, had loved the girl in the years that she had come fresh from the parish poorhouse and had brought home sweets for her and held her upon his knees, and she knew him a kind man though a rare one to ever come home. And the glass-blower, too, the way he looked upon her, full of hope. All of this past of beauty died right there as she stared at herself in the dark pool, with the fire shining bright upon her, and saw the transfiguration of herself out of the person she thought she had carried in her face.

Then, beyond her face reflected back to her, deeper within the pool, she saw a cluster of oysters bunched white in the shadow. It was almost too much to imagine putting her arm back into the cold, but she did, swearing. She grasped the oysters and yanked them up into the air, dozens of them. By the pool where she had taken them, she wrested one open with her knife and swallowed the flesh within it, and she could feel it moving down through her, living still, and cold.

She did not notice that she had cut a finger until she brought the other oysters to the fire to roast them in their shells, then she sucked upon her cut finger, savoring the salt and tang of her blood.

When the lids of the oysters rose and showed the cooking flesh within, she saw that inside some oysters there were fat pearls, which she took up in her fingers, marveling. As she held them, she saw them as though they were in the ears of haughty noblewomen, or strung and lying lu-minous on the mistress's whitened throat. And she laughed at providence handing her such precious stuff here in the wilds, where, without trade, it became trash. Yet she could not bear to throw them out but put the palmful of them into the sack, for it was as though she could feel them strung against her own skin now; and perhaps if she did at last meet the french, she could trade the pearls for food and shelter. When she thought the oysters were cooked enough, she ate them and savored them, briny and sweet, not needing to be chewed at all.

She was still cold; she would never not be cold again, she thought. She built the fire yet hotter so that it was searing the front of her gowns and her cloak but also so that her back, which faced the darkness, would be hot as well. She let the fire eat itself to smallness, and she put the warmed clothing back on her body again, layer by layer, trying to move as little as possible to prevent the lightning strikes of pain in her eyes.

Before she allowed herself to sleep, she pissed, and it hurt so much and the urine was so brown that she knew she must find water. And she crawled along on the rocks of the shore until she found a tiny spring flowing out into the bay, and filled her pewter cup again and again, drinking beyond fullness, until her throat felt less raspy and she had to piss again. It was long, her crawl back to the fire shining in the distance up the shore.

At last back, she wrapped the cloak and the two coverlets close to her and slept on the fire-warmed rock with the boat overturned and pulled over her, protected only by this, too sick and too sore to find better shelter.

Sated with oysters and egg, and warm now, her body yearned only for sleep. She slept through the night, through the embers blowing themselves out; she slept through the morning and into the late high afternoon of the fourth of the long days that she had been out wandering alone in the wilderness.

When she moved, there was so much agony in all her limbs, in her head, in her skin, that she sobbed aloud. But the way the bay was so gently touched with light made her courage return to her.

The certainty had taken root in her that if she stayed in one place for very long she would die. And yet, when she pressed herself up to her feet, the very fact of standing sickened her to retching.

She crawled along the shore until she found a pine tree with globules of pitch seeping from it, and scraped as much of it as she could with a stick upon a piece of bark, then took up the pitch; and with the stick and movements so slow that she would not jostle herself, she warmed the pitch at the coals until it was pliable, and tried to fix the places in the boat that were leaking. And then she built a little stand with driftwood in the center of the boat to keep her sack away from water that might come in, and placed her pewter cup between her feet to bail when so needed, and pushed her little boat off from the shore. And even this motion made her skull feel like it was an egg cracking open and all the juices inside running out, and she moaned aloud.

The boat picked up speed, carried by the water, and she learned to use her oar to push and row and steer.

The wind howled in her ears, terribly cold, and worked its way under her clothing down to her chilled damp skin. Her arms and back ached from the strain, but in the boat she could remain somewhat still through her journey and so refrain from further damaging her poor brains.

By the time the afternoon light lengthened and she came to shore to find shelter for the night, she had come so far from where she had woken in the morning that she marveled, for two days of walking even swiftly over the frozen ground would not have brought her so far. She felt glad of her good boat, and her body had mended just enough so that she could chew the smoked duck breast with care and keep in her stomach all of the roasted oysters that she had eaten.

She left the boat pulled up in the trees, hidden, and went deeper into the warmth of the forest, which she had missed. It felt silent inside after the loudness of the wind and water of the bay. She walked very tenderly, only a few inches each step, cautious as she was of her broken head. The deeper she moved into the woods, the warmer she felt. With careful steps and slow, she climbed a rise and came out into a little meadow shining golden in the last of the day's sun. The winter grasses there were dried a crisp silver and new green shoots were coming up, and small yellow and black birds were diving into the grasses and bursting out again, making their invisible stitches in the field.

The girl sat and watched a huge porpentine walk his bristles through the undergrowth with the weary pomp of a crowned prince and wanted to laugh but did not, for she knew laughter would hurt her immensely.

This, she thought, is one of the quiet good places of this new land.

She spread a coverlet out on a tussock of grass so plush that it was even better than the down bed that the mistress had slept upon in the city. When she lay down, she found herself bathed by the upwelling perfume of some sweet native herb. Here she was plenty warmed by the cloak and the other coverlet, and did not need to make a fire to stay free from shivering.

She summoned the ghost of the glassblower to her and felt him lying beside her upon the grass, invisible there, but she could reach out and touch him, she believed. This is the place we were meant to find, she said silently to him. This is where we would have been happy.

And she could hear, she could almost hear, the crackle of his mouth as he smiled; she could almost feel the warmth of him as his hand almost touched her hand.

She dropped into a heavy dreamless sleep and awakened in the night to discover all the stars revealed in the sky and the moon, with a chip out of its wholeness, searing bright above.

Without moving, she watched in wonder the pulsing stars above.

She listened to the nighttime noises of the forest and for the first time she felt no fear.

Something in her had been broken by that stone-throwing beast so many leagues behind her, that manlike monstrous thing; yet with the breaking, perhaps something else felt as though it were being returned by this place into a sort of harmony, a deep and humming noise within her that she hadn't understood had fallen out of tune.

The last time she saw stars so bright as these, so bold, was upon the boat in the very center of the ocean, and she lay back and felt herself upon those endless waters beneath the yet vaster sky and so awash with immensity that she found herself infinitesimal.

But now she sensed the earth under her in its spin and knew herself to be a piece of it, necessary and large enough.

For a long moment, she saw herself lying in the very center of the palm of god's hand, and the night was made of god's fingers curved to protect her against the blaze of eternity. And the stars and the moon were the space shining within. And the air felt good upon her head. The air brushed the pain out of her head with its long cold fingers.

And this felt the way it had felt when the mistress had loved her, once, when she was wondrous little and the mistress was glad to have her come to her from the parish poorhouse, for the mistress had difficulty in becoming pregnant again after her son Kit. For some sweet months, the girl had been as a daughter to the mistress.

In the poorhouse, she had been given the name Lamentations to remember the stain of her sin upon her, with her family name being Callat, so to wear upon her own neck for her life the profession of whore that her mother had almost certainly known. But when she came to the house of the mistress and her first husband the goldsmith, she began to be called many things, Girl, and Wench, and Fool, and Child, and Zed, for she was always the least and the littlest and the last to be counted like the strangest of all the letters of the alphabet.

What she remembered of the poorhouse was damp stone and loud noise and the breweries' yeasty reek and the rotten river air coming up through the windows and the cockchafer races at night performed in total silence so as not to wake the widow carekeepers and bring the floggings of shoe and switch down upon the children's heads.

She remembered fullest the times of plague, even such tiny arms as hers enlisted to hold the babies who were dying. Poor mites, she could feel them in her arms even now, with their gasping struggling breaths, each drowning to death in their own tiny lungs. Three little babies she held like this, herself only four years old or thereabouts; she held them for hours in her terrible pity even while the other children grew bored of their babies' dying and passed them around like dirty poppets or put them down and wandered off and only came back to hold their hands over the babies' mouths to see if they had died yet. But the three babies she herself held she clung to, though her arms did feel as though made of lead, until she felt the change in them when their breath ceased and whatever souls their small bodies contained escaped and drifted off toward god. She held them even when an awful stillness took their fled souls' place.

Then one day when she was four years old or five, the old minister with a face like a slab of raw beef, the one all the girls knew to hide from, came for the girl Lamentations. He shouted at her to put on a less disgusting apron and go down to the kitchen to scrub her face and hands. He growled as she scrubbed the dirt from her skin, for he was not satisfied with her cleaning; and with his sour spit upon his handkerchief, he rubbed at her until her skin was raw and she wept despite herself and said in a low voice, Nay, sir, what you see is not filth but the dye set deep in my skin.

Then he sighed and gave up and said, Now you follow me.

And she ran behind him out the doors of this, the only home she knew, and went into the muddy roads where the pigs and the kites fought over scraps, where the horses clattered by fast and terrifying huge. A counterfeit crank drooled and spasmed at their feet. And in the thicker smellier depths of the town, they had to step over a dead dog lying in the street, and her bare toe accidentally grazed the dog's side as she stepped over it; and with this lightest of touches, the dog's gassy belly burst, and all of its juices spilled from it, as wine from a wineskin spills, all over the street, and the stink of it made her vomit on her own clothing.

Upon which, the minister cursed at her and dragged her to a public fountain and bade her wash herself until she was dripping and cold. And he took her by the arm and fairly carried her the long way up to a quiet sunny street in a neighborhood of large houses, up to the door of one, where he knocked.

They were let inside a cool white space so sweet-smelling that the girl's nose drank down the smell as though it were a honeyed draught.

Through a far door, she could see back gardens full of trees and flowers. There was a conservatory, she would discover later, with lemon trees in wheelbarrows that the gardeners rolled into the outdoor sun on a fine day and back inside when there was a bite in the air. A servant wafted by and said that the mistress would see them now upstairs in the hall.

And up they went. There was a large dark door. It opened. And there the mistress was for the first time, seated in her chair with a ruff so large, so lit from behind by the sun in the window at her back, that she seemed merely a dark head upon a platter.

What is this? she said in her strange musical voice. Is it a wisp, a thought, a starveling snake?

Peer closely and squint your eyes, the minister said with a false laugh, and you shall see a strong girl, mistress. Perhaps even the dearest servant of your household. She does work hard and she knows her prayers and has an obedient heart.

Nay, said the mistress, for she is far too little even to be a turnspit. Too small for a scullion, too small to pick rags. I could not know what use such a creature may have for this household. Look upon me, child, and tell me what you are.

The girl looked up again and saw only a bloom of terror.

Nothing, she whispered.

The mistress cried, But nothing is nothing! Even so mere a mote as you is some species of thing. What exactly you are remains to be proved. And the mistress looked at the girl for a long while and made her do a little spin, and the room wobbled.

Finally, she said, A strange creature, this. Methinks I spy something moorish in her make.

And she took the girl's wrist, and later the girl understood that the mistress was marveling that the girl's skin did make her olive own seem pale in comparison, for the mistress's people had been from the darker places in Italy and were musicians in the royal courts, and though they had amassed some wealth, it could not buy them fairness beyond the lead paint they called venetian ceruse.

Aye perhaps, said the minister, but she is pretty enough. And he smiled his beef face down at the girl.

The mistress gave a sigh and waved her hand and said, Fine, I shall take her. Though what manner of servant she might be is not evident.

The mistress bargained hard then, saying that such a snip had very little use, save for eating up what food the mistress would provide. That the girl would receive bed and board and clothing. The remaining pay would go back to the poorhouse, for the mistress and minister agreed together that the widows there had done the girl a terrific service by allowing her to live to four years of age in those chill damp diseased rooms.

When the deal was done, the mistress shushed out of the room in her finery and the poorhouse minister trotted after her. The girl was left alone in the great room with its arras of a unicorn and the light that withdrew across the floor's reeds until it was swallowed up by the windows. Suddenly, before her stood a heavy dark scowling boy. This was the mistress's son Kit, whom she would watch the next day amusing himself by tugging legs off the new chicks in the pigeon house. Silently, he held out his hand. She, trusting everything in this new place, put hers into his, whereupon he took the small flesh of her wrist and twisted. She knew enough of being tiny and weak before a larger anger; the children at the poorhouse sometimes wore the brutality of the world upon their surface, so she knew not to cry out or move her face or try to snatch her arm away; she held her breath and she looked him steady in the face until a noise of approaching feet came clear. Then he stepped back into the shadows of the hall. Two marks burned on her wrist. Then the cook came in crossly with a candle that made the downy hairs upon her chin glow gold and led the girl to the kitchen, where there were green apples heaped upon the table and savory meat pies cooling there also.

The girl would discover that she had been lucky, for there had been an opening just then in the mistress's attention. Only a few days earlier, her pet monkey had gathered up his gold leash in his little paws and tiptoed out to the street and trembling awaited his trampling by a horse, for he could not take life in such bondage any longer. The mistress had been searching for a replacement pet, and soon in jest, then forgetfully, she called the girl by the poor dead monkey's name, Zed. Nay, wife, protested the goldsmith in dismay, this is unmeet, for the girl is a human child and your pet was but a fleabit monkey bought off a sailor on the wharf. But the mistress listened only to her own merry heart and it made her laugh to call the girl Zed, so the girl to the mistress became Zed, and everyone else, if they called her, strove to remember her true name, Lamentations.

And thus she became the mistress's own, her piece of a project, and the mistress in turn taught the girl many songs to sing and accompanied her on the lute, which she played beautifully because all in her family were gifted in music. She taught the girl to dance: coranto, la volta. She taught her to riddle, to use her wit; and in so teaching, she molded the girl into a delicious morsel to tempt to the house the painters and players and artists and poets the mistress so loved to call her friends.

But that first night of her fresh arrival in the house, born again out of the horrors and darknesses of the poorhouse, after the cook and another matronly servant had burnt the girl's filthy gown and bathed her with scalding water and plucked the lice and nits from her head and put her back into a fresh linen shirt that had been swiftly sewed just for her, she had fallen asleep with her head upon the kitchen table and it was the most comfortable bed she had yet known, for she was full of food and surrounded by the next day's rising bread. She woke in the night to feel the mistress stroking her cheek and opened her eyes to see the face of the mistress shining down, gilded by the candle she carried and crazed with the white paint she wore against the sumptuary laws, the removal of which she had overlooked in preparing herself for sleep that night. The mistress took the girl's hand and led her up to her own bed and allowed her to sleep at her feet upon the mattress, for she was a phlegmatic woman with slow thin blood and her feet were always cold, and she liked to warm them upon the girl's back and her soft little belly, footwarmer being as good a use as any for such a tiny bit of nothing as Zed, the mistress always said. And the girl had never before known such cleanliness or comfort or quiet, and when she woke in the morning of the next day, she was sure her ears had gone wrong. There was no sound of screaming from the babies or shouts of the children who were being beaten by the widow carekeepers for having pissed their cots in the night. Nothing but the mistress gently snoring and downstairs sounds of the servants yawning and stretching awake, and the cook in the kitchen already three hours into her day, piling the mistress's breakfast on the wooden platter and hissing at the maid to take it up to the mistress swiftly, thou lazybones good-for-nought whey-faced wanton goose.

The mistress woke then and saw the girl staring up at her with frightened eyes. She kneaded the girl's belly with her cold toes and said in a raspy voice, Do not be afeared, child. There is no one in this house who would harm you.

And the girl closed her eyes and leaned into the feet that somewhat petted her.

Just as the night wind in this place petted her and promised a safety that perhaps it could not provide. And the girl, now as then, slept.

But when she woke into a gentle fogged dawn, she saw beside her head the pawprint of a prowling cat or a wolf that had passed by in the night. The footprint was the roundness of a chamberpot, and pressed deep into the mud that had chilled in the coolness of the early morning, and it was set only inches from her head and of a size so large that it made her gasp aloud at the imagined remainder of the beast. It must have been the height of three men. Then she shook with understanding that this beast had come so near to her, had paused sniffing over her sleeping body, had perhaps been tempted, and that she would have been a very easy kill indeed. But then the beast had moved onward toward a more filling meal, and the girl was full of gladness that she was all bones and sinews with no meat at all upon her body.

She lay back again to still her swimming brain and felt her nothing of a body vibrantly alive until this newest terror seethed through her and was gone.

10.

She woke praying, O lord have mercy upon me have mercy upon me
O lord let thy mercy lighten upon me as my trust is in thee. O lord
in thee have I trusted let me never be confounded. Amen.

She packed her things slowly, considerate of her throbbing head. The
many separate pains became an all-over pain that filled her up and
made her numb. She imagined herself a mattress stuffed with husks.

She came down the slope toward the river, trying to glide, trying for
swanlike to keep the jostle low. Her sack had some nuts, a fistful of
clumped dried berries and mushrooms. Somewhere she had lost the
little basket of duck fat at her waist.

She considered eating, but the thought made waves of nausea ripple
out from her stomach into her extremities. And though she drank and
the water's cold settled in her and quieted the heat in her head, it also
made her body shudder so hard that her jaws clacked and clattered. Her

hands were as stiff as though frozen from the inside and palsied with such irrepressible force that she had a difficult time causing them to do her bidding. This quaking was so counter to her body's wishes that she knew, even as the water passed her throat, that the cold of it was doing her extreme harm.

She knelt and built a small fire and took the pewter cup and plucked some pine needles and boiled them directly in the cup until the water was brown and pungent and sharp with pine. The pine tea went down scouring and brightened her very blood; she felt it shining through her. Her shudderings calmed. Her nausea settled. She took the time to boil more and drink it all down again before deciding upon her way forward, for there was still no other way than forward, one step after another toward hope, toward salvation.

This was her fifth day in the wilds, and she longed for a roof over her head again.

The land was in such a frenzy of thawing that, though in the beginning of her flight only days earlier she had gone as swift as a bird over the frozen ground, it was now taking effort to move at all, for the mud sucked and slobbered at each boot like a child at a thumb. She slipped in walking and fell to her knees and muddied her already filthy cloak and gowns, and ripped her layers of stockings to the skin, though this pain of the bloodied knee in all the greater pains was as nothing.

Up the bay she would go once more, drawing a line against its rim, until it ended in the northernmost river that she had glimpsed on the map over the governor's shoulder. Once there, since it had seemed this river drove straight northward, she would push herself up it as far as she could go, for passage on water had proved itself superior to passage on the land during these boggy days of melt.

Again she mended what visible holes she could in the boat with a new stickful of warmed pitch, but in her dizziness, she touched the pitch with her hands and they remained defiled, her fingers thick and sticky with black stuff. She loaded her sack with its precious contents onto the little platform she'd built for it, put her own shivering body inside the boat, and pushed away from the shore. She returned with relief to the relative smoothness of the current, where, though the waves did somewhat jostle her, if she moved her body with them, they did not stir up the breathing monster of her agony.

The wind kept trying to push her this way and that, and the other shore obscured in the gray distance, and she had to paddle and push with all her might because she knew that going east was a certain death by drowning. Every so often, she bailed with the pewter cup in fear that the boat would fill with icy water and sink her, although she kept her boots up on the little stage she had built for her sack of things, so at least her feet were dry. She kept close enough to the shore that she thought if the boat were to tip, or if it were to run aground on one of the bergs of ice descending from the rivers, and she were tumbled out sudden into the water, she might still be able to bring herself to shore. She did not account for the heavy weight of her cloak and gowns and boots; she did not know that if she were to be tipped in she would drown swiftly, her limbs so stilled by cold that she would never be able to pull herself out.

She was confused by the marshes that softened the edges of the bay and made it indistinguishable from a river, the way the tides swelled in and caused strange currents that pushed her sometimes forward, sometimes backward, so she had to get out and pull the boat behind her through the shallows. When a sudden island loomed up and split the water, she often lost her sense of where she was, confusing bay for river until at last she passed the island and the water widened again. And she was always beset by the gusting winds that drove her little boat constantly forward and sideways so that she had to paddle madly to keep from being blown into shore. Perhaps worst of all, the sun, which for much of her journey had been a clear marker of direction, had become sullen, and was now hiding its face behind thick low gray clouds and would not readily show her where east was from west.

When she had a breath to consider her bearings, she tried to summon, again, the drawing of the bay she had seen over the shoulder of the governor, with the rivers radiating out of it like flares. Thinking she was moving swiftly toward the place far to the north where she believed the frenchmen might be, she tried to keep to what was the solid land on the left. But if she had been a hawk and had taken to the sky, she would have seen that, instead of staying in the bay, she had been moved by the wind and her confusion into a narrower artery, a river pouring into the bay. She thought she was moving closer to men of a familiar god to hers, to cobblestones and fruit preserves and yeasted bread. But her boat was carrying her farther from them.

It was foolish to stop to rest when her little boat was moving so sweet with the wind and the current, she thought, as if it were dancing with pleasure upon the surface of the water. And the wind cooled her head so that she was not uncomfortable now. And so, instead of pausing to stretch her cramped body or search for warmth and food upon land, she ate what she had left in the sack until there was no more food at all within it, and let herself thirst for a time. She needed to piss but held it in her. The mistress, during the coldest nights of winter, used a little brass pan from her Italian ancestors that she filled with hot stones, and on frigid days, she placed it between her bedclothes to warm them until it was time for the insertion of her own tender body between the sheets, and the girl thought of this, thought of her bladder full of hot piss becoming her own personal warming pan. And she laughed at herself, though not fully, only in breath, to keep the lightning of pain at the edge of her skull.

Once, the wind died down and the current carried her gentle for some hours. The very peace of the boat ride lulled her into a sweet contemplation as she watched the ranks of trees pass in the sun and looked upon the light as it slanted into the water. She felt a keener pleasure here, moving up the water, than she had ever felt in looking at any of the lifelike painted tableaux in the halls of the mistress's friends.

The set of her mind then became soft and infinitely open, and as she gazed down into the water, she saw in the depths below her, playing in and out of the boat's shadow, a swift great gray fish that might have been a porpoise like the ones that had danced around the ship's wake as they rode across the face of the ocean. And now it came up, came near; and there was something in the shining glimpse, the liquid black eye of the fish gazing up at her as it passed out of the shadow into the light, that made her say, Yes, aloud, and gasp. There was an element in the trembling intensity of this vision so unlike the other most dazzling moments of her life that, for a breath, it pierced the little cloud of dullness in which she normally moved through her days. And it seemed to her that she could almost see something now moving beneath the everyday, the daily, the gray and oppressive stuff of the self, something more like an intricate geometry that lived beneath the surface of the material world. And this swift and gorgeous and too-rare strike to the heart was just like when one of the goldsmith's apprentices beat and beat at a tiny lump of gold until all across the marble table on which they worked an astonishing thin leaf of gold spread outward; the vividest moments were when the leaf gently tore and one could see the cold sharp veins of the marble before the leaf was healed again by beating.

After this moment, she found herself ever so slightly changed.

She had been in her little boat for a very long while, all the chill day, when the sun began its dimming to weakness. The trees at the edge of the forest caught the light in their new tender leaves and glowed an otherworldly green. The river had narrowed enough for her to see to the other side of the banks, now shadowed and thick with darkness. She steered the boat until it ran aground, then pushed it up the shallow bank with her oar of driftwood until she could leap from the boat without wetting her boots. Then she stood with her head upon her hands, waiting for the thunder and lightning of her pain to leave her head.

Upon this somewhat dry land, the memory of the river's wind whistled in her ears and made it hard for her to listen for dangerous movement or even hear the shore's birds that were singing their sharp songs in a frenzy of mating. The agony in her bladder was such that she did not wait to piss, just crouched on the bank where she was, and she had barely lifted her skirts when out of her the brown sick piss fell hot to the ground. She was hungry, extraordinarily so. Her own fingers, having gripped the paddle of driftwood for so long, were swollen and to her eyes had begun to resemble sausages, and for a long moment, she examined them; she could taste in her mouth their savor and texture between her teeth, and after she had looked at them for a bit too long, she broke the spell by laughing at herself.

But the wind was even harsher and colder now, and this worried her. The east had been at her back for the longest part of the day, but now that she had landed and could see the whole of the sky she could see the black cloud that had slowly drawn itself over the horizon and was now dimming the sunset. She had but a short time to find shelter, she knew, before the nearing storm would crash upon her. Or else she would find herself before its wrath as vulnerable as a pink and thrashing worm.

At worst, she considered, she could crawl under the boat and wait out the storm there, but the wet would get in from underneath within a few minutes, and she thought there must be better shelter nearby, perhaps even a place where, safe from the storm, she could make a fire to warm herself and brew more medicinal pine tea and perhaps even discover something to eat.

And if, she thought grimly, she had to share a space with another dangerous stinking beast, she would have the fire and a hatchet and knife in her hands, and the sharp desperation of not wanting to die. No fleeing; she would fight this time.

And so she pressed into the forest up the incline through the brambles and thorns that snatched at her cloak and tore small holes that she would discover later, and she slipped over the mud, and as she moved her protesting body, her pain grew so large within her that she did not know how she would contain it. Inside the forest, an unnatural stillness had set in, the birds having ceased their songs of lust to find their own shelters, the beasts watching from wherever they could hide. This was a wild place and eerie, for a terrible wind must have come through not many seasons before and blown the trees down, as a great number were lying on the ground, clots of mud and even boulders caught in their exposed roots. In her fever, she felt the roots in the air in her own self, as tender as toothaches, an echoing of what she felt herself.

Then the light in the forest went a dark and angry green, and all wind, all sound, died.

Girl, hurry, and find yourself a place to hide, she said aloud.

II.

Now she rushed as fast as her poor head would allow, searching for a cave or anything at all to cover her, regretting leaving the certain shelter of the upturned boat behind; she heard something crashing through the branches above, sounding so much like a stone that she instinctively covered her broken head with her arms. But the fallen thing tumbled downward striking branch and trunk until it came to a stop at her feet, and she saw with horror that it was a chunk of ice the size of her own fist.

A thing so large falling upon her from the heavens would finish the failed job of dashing out her brains, she knew grimly.

From the sound of it, more large pieces of hail were coming down through the branches, striking the trees on the way down, making gouges in the bark, clacking and clattering and breaking with sharp cracks the branches and sticks, shaving off the vivid soft tiny leaves, making a new roar as they increased, falling not singly now but in the dozens and soon they would fall in the hundreds, and she put the sack upon her head like a helmet, as though the sack or the things within it were anywhere near strong enough to protect her, and she took to her fleetest feet despite the agony in her head and ran toward the fattest of the blown-down trees that she could see. It was a great old elm that must have been there for longer than the other trees, for the bark had been stripped from it by the weather, and the roots were as white as sunbleached bone.

She dove into the little cave under the roots, and out in the forest where she had been running just a moment before was a thickness of falling, bouncing ice.

She was protected enough from the hail here under the cave of the elm's uptorn roots, and she turned to watch the ice that sliced through the forest, rebounding upward with sprays of dirt and humus, splintered branch and leaf dust. She felt a dark pleasure, knowing that each hailstone falling was erasing her path from the land, removing her from what beast or man might be following her. When she took her hatchet in her hand and dug testingly where the tree met the ground, the wood came away easily in threads and chunks; it had been so thoroughly rotten from the dampness of the ground eating up through the wood.

With the hatchet and the knife and her bare hands, she dug a hole in the trunk deep enough to fit her body into feet first, pushing the rotted wood out to the mouth of the root-cave to build an earthworks against the elements. All around, the hail was falling to the ground, striking and leaping up, and she thought of when the fish in a pond in the springtime leapt out of the water after the skimming flies.

She took a moment to tie one of the coverlets tight to the exposed tree roots, to make a curtain against the terrifying storm outside and keep the stones from bouncing into her dim cave. In this new dark comfort, somewhat shielded from the terror, she built a fire out of the drier rotten wood and some bark and sticks that she discovered within arm's reach. Thus warmed, she wrapped herself in the second coverlet against the crawly things within the hole and inserted herself into the tree.

Through the wood she could feel, as the larger chunks of hail fell upon the trunk and rang against it, the noise drumming into her bones. But it was warm and dark and good inside the little hollow, and the noise was so loud, her body's exhaustion so complete, that she fell into a thick sleep almost instantly.

She slept as though dead, barely breathing for so long that she lost sight of day or night when she awakened. She tried to stir but could move neither arms nor legs and panicked. It was so dark that she believed herself to have been put in a coffin and interred six feet deep. I'm not dead! she cried out aloud, and she did not recognize her own voice. Then she remembered the hole she'd dug into the tree. She wormed herself wearily out. There was no scrap of warmth where the fire had been built, and she had to dig dry heart wood out of the tree to start the fire again.

When she touched the coverlet she'd hung as a curtain, it was stiff and unyielding and cold to her hand, covered to two inches thick in an armor of ice.

She knocked at the ice curtain with the back of her hatchet until it loosed, then she pushed it open to an astonishment of the world. The whole forest was glistening silver in the night. After the hail, there had been freezing rain, all of which she had missed in her depth of sleep, and the freezing rain had been halted from pouring into her little declivity by the mounds of rotted dug-out tree that she had instinctively pushed out to block the opening of her little cave. All the trees wore coats of ice so thick that they seemed glazed over with glass, and the stars shone so bright upon the world that the world shone back at the stars in stupid dazzlement.

She gasped at the vision before her, wondering; then her wonder faded into a bleak despair.

She was so hungry, and now there would be no food out there in the ice-wrecked world for her. The peppery buds of trees had been razed off by ice; the eggs newly laid in the nests would have been crushed under the ice's fists; the roots tenderly growing in the ground would have been frozen there, and when the ice melted, they would be blackened mush. The wakening spring had reverted to the desert of winter.

Morose, morose, and her eyes wept without her knowing. And there was no water for her to drink. Then she thought a bit deeper, stirring herself to pay attention, and reached out for a hailstone that had caught in some of the tree's roots, and brushed the dirt from its face, and put it into the pewter cup, then the cup into her fire. When the hailstone melted, it tasted like the forest, all moss and bark, but also of the high and furious cloud that had spat such wrath down upon her.

When she imagined putting her legs back into the rotted hole of the tree, another idea struck her, and she took a burning stick and used it as a torch and looked into the damp space there. She pushed her fingers into the soft wet wood until she saw a pale squirming and plucked a grub out of its home and held it in her palm. She watched it twisting there for a moment. Then she put it in her mouth and bit down. It tasted something of wood and something of black walnuts, and the crunch was rather satisfying, she thought, and not at all bitter as she had feared. What's more, the grub and its friends would fill her hungry stomach. And so she searched along the rotted wood and slowly filled the pewter cup with grayish grubs, all squirming like babes, and she closed her eyes when she put them in her mouth for they were revolting to look upon, but she ate them all down. And her stomach was glad. And the pain in her head quieted its bellowing exigencies and gave her a small peace now.

Her fire had warmed her little cavern enough to have melted the majority of the coverlet's ice. She caught the drip in her cup and drank it down; over and over she drank, slaking her thirst until she had to back her bare rear out into the icy world to piss upon its radiant midnight shine. Then she returned to her rotten hollow in the tree and allowed her body to sleep for the rest of the night.

When she woke, she could barely see the little red bird that stood in a slender opening of the coverlet, a small form against the shock of morning light on the world encased in ice.

The bird hopped inside. It looked at the girl with its buttony black eye. It opened its beak.

O you, girl, the bird said gently. Is it time? Do you give yourself up?

To what? the girl thought at the bird.

To the release of your immortal soul from this base bodily form, the bird said. To meet your longed-for beloveds in the kingdom of heaven.

There will be no heaven for me. I am not of the elect, the girl thought.

You will not be the final judge of your soul, the bird said.

And it took the girl a very long time to think this over. The bird quivered, watched her with one shining black bead of an eye. The girl came to a decision, and at last she said, No. Not yet.

The bird gave a sigh and hopped back up into the brilliant slit in the day and extended its wings and flew off. And back into sleep the girl fell further.

12.

The old night terrors now rushed through her dreams.

She saw a flat gray pond in which there was growing a glob like a man's hawked spittle. The mass pulsed at its edges and began to glow an unnatural green.

Something screamed from nearby, invisible but so shrill, so loud, that she felt the wind of the scream upon her body, which she discovered, with a sick horror, was crouched at the edge of the strange pool and as naked as a newborn babe.

Overlapping with this first came another, an ever more ancient night terror that she had known well, in which there was a deep purple sky cracked and crazed with lightning as though it were falling into pieces, and she was running, running away, and what was chasing her was so horrid that her brain slipped in panic from understanding what it could be, but she could feel it behind her, nearing in on her, its breath and its steps on the ground beneath her own flying feet; it was catching up; in a moment it would leap upon her.

And the primordial night terrors overlapped in swift frenzy with the terrors from her actual life, badness against badness, sliding.

And here she was again in the mistress's house, and they were standing at the window of the solar room that leaned out over the street, and the scullions had brought in fresh reeds for the floors and scattered handfuls of sweet herbs here and there, and the scent of lavender and thyme and rosemary and lemon balm rose and filled her head, for Kit, the mistress's son, was coming home from the university and was bringing with him four noble friends.

And suddenly, here they were, coming up the street on horseback with Kit's white greyhounds like tiny horses trotting behind. The mistress gave a cry of joy and settled herself in her chair where the dimness was most flattering to her age and said, Quick, quick, Zed, fix my paint. Then, as the noises of the boys coming stomping in from downstairs rose to them and the servants loudly greeted them, the girl took the brush and touched up the white lead paint on the mistress's skin, her face and neck and the greater part of her exposed breasts, then powdered the whole, then the mistress covered her bosoms insufficiently with a fine silken partlet and her largest whitest stiffest ruff. Then the girl dabbed carmine on the mistress's cheeks and lips, patted stray hair back under the pins, and dropped belladonna in her eyes so that the mistress's pupils leapt up and swallowed her irises. And the mistress waited, panting gently, elegantly draped over her fine carved chair, and the girl stepped behind her mistress and folded her hands upon her stomach and attempted to hide herself in what darkness she could discover between the fine arras of the unicorn and the wall on which the arras was hung.

Now a clattering up the staircase, and the boys burst into the room, laughing at some joke between them. Then the friends went silent, looking in wonderment at the mistress, whose beauty was renowned well beyond the city, even all the way to the university town. It was also known, perhaps, that the goldsmith, the mistress's husband and the father of Kit and the child Bess, was extremely aged and palsied, and had begun to lose his mind and that not long from now the mistress would perhaps be a widow of very weighty wealth indeed. And the boys were dazzled by her and by the prospect of her future rich widowhood as well.

Kit recognized this perhaps and a bad flush came over his face, and he gave a low sardonic bow and said, Mother.

You have come, his mother said in her lilting musical voice. You are all welcome, young gentlemen. You must be hungry from your travels. Your rooms are prepared for you and I have had hot water on the boil for hours now so that you might freshen yourselves up before supping.

Kit's tongue darted out of his mouth and dabbed pink at his lips. We require, Mother, a servant of our own to do our bidding. And he looked at the girl, his mother's little pet, standing behind her mistress, and smiled. We shall be wanting a great deal of running and fetching.

O, said the mistress, yes, well, I shall ask the newest maid to wait upon you. She is a good matronly widow and strong.

No, no, he said, We want her. And the girl saw with horror that he was pointing at her hiding in the shadows. Your little Zed. She is ever so clever and so nimble, and none of the other maids have the brains to learn the latin we are to speak over these weeks if we are to grow better at ease in the language. Only your little parrot has the mind for it. As well, we shall be requiring entertainment, and here's a pretty little thing to sing and dance for us. For you have trained your little pet so well that she reflects so beautifully upon you.

And one of the other boys gave a chuckle, and the girl could feel five pairs of eyes feeding upon her.

She had a sense as though she were sinking through the wood then the mud of the ground, that the floor was crawling up her knees, her thighs, her groin. And even with her eyes lowered, she could feel the mistress's gaze flicking on her face, and upon it, the girl put a firm no.

No, the mistress said. She is not for you. For your sister the child Bess does need Zed to clean and comfort and teach her during the days, and as a doting brother, you would never deny your sister her nurse-maid and sweet companion.

Ah, Kit said. But I must insist, for we are here for such a short time, only a fortnight, and the child Bess will surely find far better instruction at her mother's knee. Of course, if you are unwilling, we could easily visit my father, your husband and master, at the goldsmiths' guildhall, for he can refuse his dear son nothing.

The girl felt the mistress struggle within her cool unmoving self, but too soon the woman gave up. She said, Fine, fine, you may have her, but she is not to be teased as you boys do tease.

Now in the girl's direction Kit sent his acid look, then the five boys poured out of the drawing room, making riotous noise, and they went to the dining table, where the cook had already set out the meat pies and salats. The girl slowly followed behind them, feeling terror scrabbling about in her.

The mistress seized her hand as the girl passed, and hissed, Be sage, my child, use your wiles, do not find yourself in the room with them when they are drunk, do not allow them liberties.

And the girl tried, she did; she used her wits and was good and quick and dodged hands and feinted to draw their attentions away from her neat pretty person. She laughed off their words; in exigency she learned their latin as swift as they spoke it, and spoke it back to them, and they marveled at her, this unlettered scrap of a servant, picking up things that the sharpest among them struggled with. She learned to keep to the edges of the room where there was less light, to keep a door always a step away, to foresee their needs so that they would not have to call for her and would thus forget that she had been lent to them. She would become, she imagined, a creature of air, invisible, to be summoned for her magic then disappear.

After they fell drunkenly into their beds late in the night or in the morning, Zed crept off to sleep a few hours, exhausted, still in her dress in case they might summon her out of her sleep to bring them water or wine or ink or paper or bread and butter or whatever else they required.

Bring us hot chestnuts, they shouted in their latin, take off our boots, girl, fix this tear in my cloak, and quick, wash my stinking stockings, fetch the apothecary for this sot has drunk so much it seems he cannot stop in his vomiting, clean up this vomit for it is everywhere, it stinks in here, open the windows, what a pig, what an addlebrains, bring us a basin, bring us more mead but the good mead this time, make it quick, make it quicker, thou dusky lazy slattern, thou paltry shrimp, bring us the bathwater, bring us the soap, bring us a better towel, bring us the sponge, the aquavitae, the wine, the beer, the bread, the books, not this book thou blinking antic, canst thou not read? O ho! Not a jot can she read, is it? Well, and yet so quick to pick up latin, what marvels this little creature contains, someday one of us must teach the dumb zany her alphabet. Bring us oranges, what remains of the venison stew from lunch for the greyhounds, remove this shit the blasted animal left upon the floor, bring us the whetstone, pamphlet, pen, lamp, candles; bring us more wood for the fire, more scent for this room does reek, bring us the lute of my mother and all the cushions in the household for our heads. Wake up wake up thou lazy wench, thou stupid slut, thou nimble mischance, thou collop of mince, thou sooty mammet, why dost thou sleep when a man needs thee? Come this way, be silent, do not with thy questions wake the house, mind, but make thy coming quick for we are drunk and the night is old and soon the cocks shall crow and the servants stir to waking. And we do not wish the sun awake to watch our will be done. For, girl, thou must in thy quietest voice sing us a song now, no, a prettier song, for such a pretty pretty mouth should certainly sing prettier songs. Now thou shalt dance for us. Softer now, thou toothsome grub, thou tawny bead. Now jail thy tongue. Now deaf thine ears. Now shut the door and put a chair against it. Now we are cozy within, are we not? Let us see what thou hast under this pretty dress of common stuff.

And there was no way out of the room, though she was then near to the window and considered the jump. But it was a long three stories to the sand garden in its patterns below, and the night made the fall seem endless and mortal.

Be not afraid, girl, one said kindly.

Bring thy small and lovely person over to me, one said.

O hush now, thou knowest that nobody would come to thee if thou wouldst shout, Kit said.

Only in her sleep did she struggle and cry out as she had not done then, but the damp wood of her hovel in the tree absorbed her motion and the kicking of her heels.

The dream jerked, and she was staring into the polished metal mirror at the mistress's face as she put the mistress's newly blackened hair up with pins. And the mistress sighed and leaned into her hand and said, Ah but the house feels so dead now without those dear boys in it. I hope that they have arrived back at the university in good health and good weather.

A bitter darkness welled up in the girl, and she said in the latin the boys had taught her, Ubi mors ibi spes.

Then the mistress clucked her tongue and said crossly, Thou knowest well that I do not speak latin, my Zed, what on earth could this mean?

Then the girl let the mistress's heavy black hair fall from her hands and said, It means that should any one of them set foot in this house again, I shall gladly put poison in their wine and go to the gallows a murderess.

She braced for the strike of the boar-bristle brush upon her cheek, but the mistress did not strike her. And when she looked up, she saw the mistress's face gone still as she looked at the girl's own face in the glass, then she turned and put a hand up to the girl's cheek.

Ah, child, she said. Thou hast suffered, but take comfort that thou hast suffered only the daily lot of woman. Do not think for a moment that this pain I have not known myself. And take solace also in this, that though thou hast sinned, I could not imagine that the gracious lord would not forgive thee for thy sins. For thy will had been overrun; it was not thy heart that held desire in it, and thine was the lesser sin of all.

Well, the mistress amended after having turned around. It would be a lesser sin if there should remain no issue born out of the unfortunate event.

Then she thought some more and told the girl to have the cook brew up a strong kettle of tansy, which the girl should drink today and every day, and nothing but tansy tea for a week.

The girl woke to these dark thoughts and rolled them around her head. It was true that she had sinned that night, the last of the boys' stay. But of course it was not the sin of what her body had been forced to do that gnawed upon her; her only true sin then was that the whole time it took place she was dreaming of murder.

O father, forgive my sins, for my heart has been bitter and wrathful and full of hatred. One day more of those boys' company and there would have been one fewer gentleman scholar up at the university. She was sure of it. Perhaps even a handful fewer. For she knew where in the pantry the rat poison was kept. She knew the soft places in the belly to stick a knife, for, when at the poorhouse, she had one day been peering out a window and saw a man on the street punch a knife into the guts of another man, who crumpled to the street, instantly dead.

She groaned and pulled her body from the hole in the tree trunk and went to the wet hanging coverlet and pushed it open to the day. The sun shone swords into her head, and she winced. She had sweated through her gowns in the warm hole in the log, and now she put her wrists out upon the melting ice on the earth and held them there through the burn on her skin until her blood cooled. She took an icicle that descended prettily from one of the dangling roots and touched it to the bony bump upon her head until this, too, felt less tender under the numbing cold.

She poked her head outside again. For some time, she kept her eyes closed against the sharpness of sun, but she slowly opened her lids, one then the other. The world was all ablaze with ice, the world was on fire with ice. She could hardly bear it.

There was a tremendous crack then in the near distance, and she cowered to the ground, for it was precisely the sound of a musket firing upon her, and she thought in frenzy of one of the men of the fort who had somehow tracked her over the wilds to this place.

But then she saw in the clearing at the top of the hill that there were trees so bowed under the weight of ice that at last it was too much for the trees to bear, and one by one they gave a shiver and all at once exploded outward, one after the other, in a line along the ridge, snapping back against the ice and sending up shimmers of ice splinters into the air, which formed golden clouds as they caught the light and drifted off in a great high shining fleece into the wind.

It would be too perilous to move under the exploding trees, let alone under the thick skin of ice that would make her slip and fall and succeed at last in killing her with a new blow to the head. She must stay where she was to let the bones of her skull knit themselves together, and eat as many of the grubs as she could wrest out of the rotten wood and try to regain some of the strength her flight had stolen from her.

13.

The girl knocked down another icicle and put it into the pewter cup near the embers of her fire. She took the hatchet to hack at her hole, making it both larger and deeper to feed the fire alive again. There was a dry wood farther in that made the fire burn hotly, and she stacked it by the entrance for later use. She spent a while gathering grubs and eating them and even tried a kind of plenteous spider with filaments for legs, but the spider was sour and unsatisfying, and she let the rest of them scurry away from her hand.

She also tasted the moss that grew near the base of the felled tree, and found it edible. She tried to scrape off the inside of what bark was left on the sides of the trunk with her teeth, the way the mistress had eaten the flesh off the leaves of the strange mace-headed artichokes she so loved, but this bark provided a tiny and very bad meat.

At her leisure now, she could unpack her sack and care for her items again, polishing each to better health. The hatchet had pine sap embedded deep in its handle, which she scraped off with the knife. The sack had opened some tiny holes, and thus alarmed her, for it meant that the food she put in it might escape, so she took threads out of her fraying hem and carefully pierced tiny holes with the tip of the knife to sew the threads through and close the holes. The boots were in the worst shape, the nail having come through the heel entirely and a mouth having opened at the large left toe between the sole and the leather. She patched them with what she could, pitch and straps of her underdress, more cuttings from the coverlet, moss, wadding, then she polished them and put them near the fire to fully dry.

Good boots, she said aloud. Protect your health and be obedient now, for we must go far before we come to a place of safety.

Then all of her things shone back at her as though they were smiling.

She smiled back upon them, for she loved them better than she loved most humans, for these things were her only friends and were only eager to serve her.

When all was neat and cared for, the girl did not know what else to do, for she could not remember a single day of her life that she was not burdened with thousands of tasks, and now her hands were empty as she waited for the melting of the world. Beyond the many duties she performed for her mistress, it was the child Bess who was her primary concern, born when the girl herself was only four or five and not long arrived in the household. The girl Zed had been there at the harrowing birth when the mistress had bundled the babe up, was the one who had held the screaming newborn in her arms while the bloodied filthied sheets were taken out and fresh ones put on and the mistress placed into a new nightgown. And the girl had looked down at this clenched red fist of the child Bess's face and felt helpless and moved; she had never seen anything so gorgeous and so revolting in her four years, nothing so purely good and purely animal as what had taken place in the birthgiving. She had loved the child Bess with all her soul from that moment, ferociously, for everything, for her softness and her vulnerability and the child Bess's raw need of the girl herself.

Only she and the mistress and the midwife, who was bribed with gold to forgetting, knew of the child Bess's shocking red birthmark of a face with horns pressed upon the babe's thin chest. Luckily so, too, for if they had been known of, the devil-mark and the brainlessness together would have filled the whole household, then the whole street, with the superstition of the infant being born under a demonic curse; and her life like that of the household entire would have been far harder than it was.

In any event, the child Bess, as she grew, became the girl Zed's poppet, her plaything, her sister, her charge, her daughter, her nearest companion in her bed. Hers was not a labor of serving but rather a labor of adoration, and thus almost no work at all, and she carried the babe about and kept her dry and clean, and brought her to the wet nurse and rocked the babe to sleep; but her labors were still constant and needful, for the wet nurse was a terrible drunk and unreliable for anything but milk, and the mistress a most uninvolved mother. The goldsmith might have been a doting parent, but he was rarely in the house, rising before dawn, setting off to the goldsmiths' guild, for he loved his work more than anything in the world, and his fingernails were rimmed all around with gold dust. When he finished his work, he went to the taverns to eat and drink and listen to the talk, and came home for only a few hours of sleep before waking and setting off to work again. And so it was the girl who saw the child Bess's first step, very late, at near three years old, she who taught the child what small language she had rattling round in her head. It was she who went a ghost through the house at night, returning things to their proper places that the child Bess had stolen throughout the day, the hairpins and baubles and her mother's jewels, the unripe apricots off the tree, the pig's teeth from the hearth, the flowers crushed in her hand. For, like a clough, the girl took for herself what she thought beautiful and decorated her little bed with these things. They had named the child Bess after the queen of the realm who was shrewd and bold and gingery and beautiful, hoping that some of those virtues would rub off on the babe. But a more unlike creature to the queen had never been born in england.

Still, as the mistress said in her rare moments of tenderness toward her daughter, though she be but paltry in her mind and spirit, it is true that our own Bess grows her gold from her crown, not the inverse.

And the child Bess did have the most luxuriant locks of silken shining hair; it was her glory.

But all of the child Bess's strength went into that hair, and no other strength was left behind. Still, though she had a sparse handful of words, her constitution was sunny, and she would spend long hours in the garden, laughing at the way moths zigged in the air and zagged through the flowers, her wet red mouth gaping open and making all the stableboys gaze upon her, though they knew they should not. It took some searching for a stranger to know what manure she had in her

brains, for she kept quiet and smiled, and her face and hair were so astonishing beautiful that all went silent before her, and the mistress,
when she could be bothered to look upon her daughter, would smile
bitterly and say, Well, we shall marry my daughter to a rich old noble-
man, for they love their girls pretty, fair, and monstrous stupid. And
the child Bess would grin up at her mother with her pink mouth open
and drooling, her teeth already rotting from the sugar she so loved and
stole in fistfuls from the cook, who pretended not to notice her clumsy
creepings in the pantry and who left small treats here and there for her,
though she had been forbidden to.

So deep in thinking of the lost child Bess, the girl did not notice until midday that the melt of the ice had begun in earnest. The trees poured
water down their trunks and rained it from their branches, and streams
of shining ice-water opened up all through the woods and rushed down
to the river below. She kept her body as perfectly still as she could and
rose only to boil water to drink it down and in so doing warm herself.

The soreness in her body from her six days running was such that
she felt infinitely older than her years, a wizened hag, and she knew
that, even should she have long months of only rest, there had been
things in her body that had been changed forever. She was but sixteen
or seventeen or perhaps eighteen years of age, but the wilderness had so
moved upon her that she would never be young again.

The night stole in and she ran out of wood to burn, but it did not matter.
The world was so warm and her log-hollow and coverlet and fever were
sufficient to keep the cold away, and she slept well.

She woke when the night was still heavy on the forest, and lit one tarry branch she had pulled off a nearby pine, and by its small light, she gathered what grubs she could. She pressed moss in the mouth of the pewter cup to keep the grubs in their place. Then she wrapped all her things up in the sack, and tied it to her body under her clothing, and took two sturdy sticks to balance herself, and moved down the still-dark hillside slowly in all the wet and the mud. She had hidden her boat well enough in the trees during the onrushing storm, and it had been protected somewhat from the apocalypse of hail. She found no hail-holes in it, to her astonishment. She gave thanks aloud in her cracked voice, for the boat was still willing to carry her.

As the sun poured over the east, she paddled herself up the river with her oar of driftwood. After the long span of morning, the effect of the ice storm was less visible from the forest rushing by on both sides; there were no broken branches or trees stripped of their buds, and the streams were no longer roiling with meltwater. It seemed these woods had not known hail so recently; it seemed that the hail had been a freak finger of ice in the clouds poking inland from the ocean, pointing down at the girl herself. And though it felt as if she had been personally chased, she was glad for the new rush of trees with their merry green budding, for the birds weaving constant in the air here.

14.

She had to stop to stretch her legs at midday. They had been so cramped by the boat that it had begun to feel like knife blades had been embedded in her thighs. She chose a flat gray rock that seemed like the sun would have warmed it, and pulled her boat up on it after her. The wind was so strong in this place that she could hardly stand in it, and it rummaged under her clothes and grated at her cheeks and chilled her thoroughly.

She looked around her upon the shore to see what kind of food might be near, and after some wandering, she found a strange short longleafed tree with a few of last year's fruits hanging in brown dried dugs from it. She took one and stripped the skin off and tried a sliver of its flesh, and it was sweet and not immediately poisonous and was not even poisonous after she ate a bit more and waited. So she picked what she could of the dried dug-fruits and put them in her sack.

————

The knowledge had begun circling in her; now its circles were so tight and swift that she could no longer ignore it, that she had somehow strayed from the bay, that this water she was on was a river, and that it was not the northernmost river on the map that the governor had stabbed with his stubby finger, for it seemed all morning the sun was warming her back and her left side, which meant she was heading northwest. But everything that had come before the hovel with the grubs and the hailstorm was a fevered dizziness to remember, and she could not quite see where she had gone awry.

She felt low then, low and sad.

She did not know if it was better to turn her boat around and try to find the bay again or press on deeper into the thick of this vast and wild country and perhaps see that the river bent pure northward.

While thinking, she built a fire to warm herself, and staring into the puddles by the shore, she saw some crayfish darting along the stones and was quick enough to catch four of them, though they pinched her fingers with their little claws. And one pinched the wound she'd cut deep into her finger with the oyster shell and made it smart and ache. She roasted the four crayfish in the fire until their shells screamed, and peeled them when they were cool enough to touch, and the flesh was good and sweet and melted on the tongue. But this was not nearly enough. She was still monstrous hungry. She filled her mouth with some of the dried dug-fruit and the remainder of the grubs out of the pewter cup and thus she sated herself.

———

She returned to the boat, to the river that had dimmed itself in her disappointment that it was in fact a river. It was perhaps foolish, she did not know; but she would follow it, she had decided. She felt lucky that the wind was blowing so strong upon her back.

The boat had begun to take in much more water than before, and she had to bail with the pewter cup frequently now. Though she had raised her feet out of the water, her hems had draggled in it; and the fabric soaked up the chill and licked cold at the backs of her thighs.

Still, she pressed on because she sensed that such a strong wind would not be at her service every day and that when springtime had fallen fully upon this land the wind would calm and the press of it would relent and she would find it harder to make her way up the river.

All was shimmering blue now, dark water and the grackles circling above in the daylit sky.

Late in the afternoon, being pushed by the wind close to the riverbank, she saw in passing two small children of the people of this place crouched over something moving upon the bank. She held her breath, for this was the first waking view of human beings that she had had since she had fled the fort, for surely the beast-man who had stoned her did not count. The children were so interested in the thing at their feet that they did not see her, and when at last some noise of water lapping upon the hull reached them and they looked up, they blinked and gaped at her as though they could not believe they were seeing this strangeness before them. She smiled weakly and raised a hand to prove her harmlessness. She passed only twenty feet beside them and saw that the children were playing with a wolflike dog whelp that was tugging at the end of a stick one of the children was holding. The whelp saw the girl passing and dropped its end of the stick in astonishment and gave a shrill yap.

The girl slid shushing by in her boat. She craned her neck around to watch the children, who stood staring until she was lost to them around a bend in the river.

And when she was gone from their sight, she suddenly saw herself as if using the eyes of the children who had watched her passing, and what she saw was a brittle sticklike figure, itself not obviously human, in a crude carved log. Her darkish face in the shadows of the cloak's hood would not have been visible to them. Perhaps the children thought they had seen a ghost passing. Perhaps they felt wonderment, awe. Perhaps, she thought, they would return to their village and tell their mothers hesitantly that on the river this morning they had watched a faceless ghost pass upon the water; perhaps she would enter into the stories that these children would tell through their lives, and then this quick vision of her, the tiny glimpse, would be passed from person to person among the powhatan people down through generations.

The girl smiled to imagine some part of her surviving her own body's decline and death.

But in fact, as the bend of the river swallowed the girl in the boat, the children looked one at another and they laughed. There was no awe here. The madness of the woman in the boat was so forceful that it was like the rays of the sun; the children felt it touching them even where they stood. A living skeleton she was, the boat so ungainly it was like a flipped beetle waggling its helpless legs, a ridiculous sight.

And the two girls laughed and laughed until their stomachs hurt, and the whelp leapt up at their faces, overexcited by the noise.

Then the older girl sighed and wiped her face with her palm and said to her little sister that one of them should run and tell the mothers up planting the maize in the high fields that they had seen the mad wandering woman that the runners who had come into the village a few days earlier had told them about. That the little sister should do it because her legs were swifter.

But the little sister was no longer as tractable as she had been when she was smaller, she had begun resisting the orders of her older sister, and she sat heavily on her bottom and scratched a bite on her arm and said irritated that she would not go because, if she did, their mother would put her to work. And the older sister tried to pull her little sister up by the arm, but the younger knew how to make herself heavy and boneless, and though the older sister was a head taller, she could not budge her younger sister.

At last, the older sister shouted that, fine, she would go, but she was going to take the puppy with her because the puppy loved her more. And the little sister said she didn't care, but she only said this because she thought that the puppy would stay with her, for obviously it loved her more. But when the older sister ran off, the puppy ran with her and now the little sister was left all alone on the bank.

She became bored, then she became angry in her loneliness because there was no one to play with, only the wind ruffling the face of the river. Soon, though, she heard a cheeping noise and scooted to a hole in the bank where she saw the blue crown of a kingfisher mother who was frantic to draw the girl away from her puffy new chicks. Before long, the smaller girl, making peeping noises at the chicks so that they showed her their fine pink throats, forgot all about the stranger in the boat entirely and would not think of her again in her life.

At dusk, the girl allowed herself to tumble out of the boat and lie on the riverbank, panting with fatigue.

The river had narrowed and gone around a jagged promontory, and the forest here was thicker and full of vines. It was too late for her to find shelter before nightfall, so she contented herself with cutting soft pine boughs to sleep on beneath the boat and building a wall of rock to hide her fire, for she was exposed here on the riverbank to whatever eyes might be about. She had not eaten since midday and was too tired to hunt for more food. She chewed on the brown leather of the fruit until it softened and slipped down her throat, but could manage only a few mouthfuls before sleep stole over her, the leathered fruit still in her hand.

She was up, racked with shivers in the cold before dawn, and in the boat moving northward as the east sparked with light. She paused once at midday and discovered good walnuts in the humus beneath a tree and put as many as she could in her sack, then she went on and paused again for the night just as twilight poured dark over the land, and she discovered a clutch of pigeon eggs, which she sucked down without cooking.

Three days passed on the river like so, the hard wind keeping up and the boat covering her body like a coffin at night, the same small fire to dry her boots, the light of which she hid with a wall of her hands' making.

On the fourth day, a low cold mist settled over the land, and she felt somewhat hidden on the river from any eyes that were there to watch her pass.

She frighted a fish out of the mouth of a crane and ate it. She scurried and caught a handful more crayfish. She ate buds off the trees and the nuts and dried fruits she held in her sack. She found at the river's edge purple plums like the ones she knew from home but they were sour and sparse and dried up from the winter.

She became so hungry that she tried to eat the softer clumps of dried mud at the edge of the forest, for they looked somewhat mushroomy, but she chewed them and spat them out before swallowing and was left with a meaty film upon her tongue.

On the fourth night, on the path returning with dry firewood in her arms, she saw a mother doe and her fawn ahead of her. She bent slowly to lay the wood down and seize a rock. The doe heard her and wheeled around. And though deer are known for their gentleness and fleetness, if the girl had moved even slightly, this mother deer would have charged her, would have knocked her down and trampled her, kicking, it was so large and so fierce. The girl froze with the stone in her hand. In a flicker of two white tails, the deer, large and tiny, now sailed into the dim gray woods and were gone.

In her fury, the girl threw the stone after them and hit only a tree. For a long time afterward, her mouth could not stop salivating, because if she had knocked the fawn down, she would have fallen on the tender creature and eaten its flesh without even cooking it; she was so starved, she would have chewed down the tender bones. She imagined it over and over until she could taste the babe's dark rich blood upon her tongue.

In the wake of the deer's flight, the forest felt newly lonely.

She began sleeping longer to avoid her hunger, and even in her sleep, her body began to quake so tightly that she drummed her knees and elbows against the upturned boat in a constant rattle, which in her dreams returned as a kettle on a hot fire boiling and shuddering its handle against the iron hanger.

When she was on the river, it narrowed even more, opened up again, now sometimes was walled on one side or the other with large gray stones, and sometimes seemed to be splitting into separate rivers on the opposite side, but these were only islands, and around them, the water healed itself.

On the sixth day after the ice storm, she could only with pains bring herself to her feet. They jostled out from under her and seeming danced to no music at all.

It was only when the girl tried to move forward that she understood that the pain she was feeling was not simply coming from where the stone flung by the beast-man had struck her or from the many wounds she had sustained in flight. It was blooming outward from within. It was a fever that had begun with a spark and was now radiating its heat all the way from the bone out of the pores of the skin.

Something had wrested the fever out of its latency in her marrow; or perhaps it was simply the harsh end of winter rubbing its cold body up against her starved worn body.

Nevertheless, a fever was, she knew, a very bad thing. She had seen many a fever in her time. The flush, the glassy eyes, the brains cooked into madness.

The fever was the ocean in her, waves rising and troughs falling under her skin.

Her broken head pulsed all the way down her spine to her tail-bone.

The birds of the sky spun too quickly in her sight and their song rasped upon her ears.

When she did manage to put the boat in the river with all the effort she could muster, it glided down the rocky bank and sank to the bottom before she set a foot in it.

She sat for a long time upon a rock and dumbly watched the boat as it rested against the shallow riverbottom. Out of the wood came a thin trail of dirt and dead insects and tiny bubbles of air, which oiled the surface in a swirl, then drew thinly off down the current.

Was she weeping? she asked herself. She touched her cheeks and found them cold and wet, but perhaps it was the dampish wind upon her.

———

She watched her breath leave her body in puffs of smoke.

An eagle, as large as a horse, circled in the sky against scurrying low clouds and threw its trembling shadow against the shining face of the river.

Goodbye, my sweet boat, she said aloud. Thou hast been a goodly servant and I did love thee well.

The boat glowed darkly from the bottom of the river, as though relieved to be allowed to revert to dead wood.

She took the driftwood paddle, which had chapped and blistered her and moved her many leagues, and which in turn her own bleeding hands had polished to a smoothness and a shine, and she leaned upon it as her staff to help her over the rocky wet terrain ahead.

A staff, she thought, was the sign of a pilgrim.

There was pleasure in this thought. A pilgrim wound his way to sacred lands for the salvation of his soul.

And not long after, over the wet and slopping ground, she remembered that a staff was also a sign of an old person, an unsteady person. A person only a few steps away from death.

15.

Still, it was a relief to come into the forest to escape the scourings of the wind.

Each step pained her in the bones of the legs and the fever in her head.

She stopped at streams to drink and trick her stomach into believing itself full, then continued on, leaning upon her staff.

She dreamed of her dutchboy glassblower, imagining him just there behind her, his good calm quiet self, the strength in his shoulders, his pretty watchful face. She dared not look behind herself for the sorrow of not seeing him there; in her fever, she preferred to imagine her living body trailing his ghost behind it like a mist, like breath made visible.

We will get to where we are going, she said to him aloud, and I will keep you alive in my heart.

We will come to a place of salvation, she said to him, and I will sit in a church and pray for your soul.

We will arrive and we will eat hot bread, endless hot bread, and we will not stop eating, she said to him, until one day, when we are very old, we will die of too much eating.

And it was all right that he did not answer her when she said these things, for of course he hadn't ever spoken her tongue.

Now the sound of the river became harsher upon its rocks, and she thought somewhat sluggishly, in the hot fog of her brain, that perhaps this meant there would be rapids nearby.

She picked down over the bank and saw a frothing of white up the long stretch of river. There was spray in the air, and she could see quick spangles of silver flashing above, then winking out.

Because her thoughts were thick in her head and wondrous slow, only after a long while did she understand that the spangles were leaping fish in their spawning, diving up the current, and enough of them that they might be simple to catch.

She went as fast as her hitched and limping gait allowed, and started first a fire, for she knew that in her fever and starved state she could not bear the cold water for long. Then she dropped her stick and removed her cloak and sack and outermost gowns and boots and what stockings remained that were not but bloody threads stuck deep into the wounds of her feet and legs.

And then she carried her tender shocked body into the hard cold of the water, and in her hand, she held her knife.

Her feet ached differently here, the new variety of pain something like relief.

She shuffled to a place behind a stone, safe from the hard push of the rapids, where the weary fish were gathering their strength to attempt their next leapings. The water was so strong that it nearly swept her away, and she took hold of a boulder to catch herself. If her legs went out from under her, the rapids would dash her against the rocks; the rocks would gnash at her already tender skull.

There she moved very little until the fish forgot that her legs were not of the river, and they lost their wariness. She found a large one that seemed sleepier than all the others and let it come near, then she darted and stabbed it hard through the head; and though its tail thrashed and pummeled her forearms and it strained to free itself with nearly more force than she herself held in her own wasted body, she carried the fish with care up the banks, leaving a set of footprints made bloody by the river-rocks chewing upon her wounds. On the dry land, she clubbed the fish with her driftwood staff until the fish was dead. Then she replaced her cloak over her shivering form and warmed herself by the fire until she could use her limbs again, and gutted the fish, only barely halting herself in the extremity of her hunger from putting the guts into her mouth to eat them. Then she cooked the fish upon the spit. As it was cooking, she replaced her clothing, hot from the fire and delicious on her scoured skin.

She wrapped both of her coverlets around herself and loved them dearly for their comfort. She ate some fish that was not yet cooked and was so hungry that it was like hot water to her and had seeming no taste at all.

Knowing from bad experience that intemperate eating did make her vomit, she forced her hands still in her lap as she waited, singing three songs through under her breath.

And when, at the end of these, the fish still had not finished cooking, she imagined, as in a vision before her, the stretch of silver street from noble to addle in the city back home and placed herself walking in the morning light there and running her hands over the plaster or stone or wood of each house as she went past the small unremarkable church and the goldsmith's and the saddler and the letter-writer and the milliner's shop with its pretty linen cap with peak and side wings in the front window, which only showed itself fly-speckled when you peered closely past the dirt on the panes of glass. The smell of city smoke, of bodies, of piss against the walls. This way she forced herself to remember what came next and next and next, and she even skirted the beggars in the road, No-Hand-John who held his earthen cup up between his stumps and the woman who threw her baby at passing men to get them to catch it so she could pick their pockets. And only when the girl was back in the city so thoroughly that she heard the bell of silver street as though she had summoned it did she take the fish from the fire and eat the flesh down. She tried to slow herself but was still hungry when she finished the last of the fish.

And so she called her courage to return to her and took off her clothing and went back into the water and, shivering, caught another fish. Then she wandered her city in her head until the fish was cooked and, bite by bite, ate the entire second, including the cheeks and both eyeballs.

Then she lay down, for her body would not obey her commands any longer, so occupied was it with dealing with the fish inside her. And the fever-clouds that had fallen over her brain faded somewhat from where she was lying, and she saw what her deep pain could not allow her to see before, that the day was full of sunlight and blue skies and red and white flowers in their very earliest buddings at the tips of the trees. O, she thought, she had allowed the beauty of this world to be swallowed by her hunger, by her fever. And she was glad now, for she had walked herself beyond the end of winter, for this was fully the good and fruitful spring.

The day had lengthened into early afternoon when she could move her body once more, and she made the fire larger and hotter to warm herself, then she took off all her clothes and, full naked, went in again and stabbed two fish just moments before her shuddering became so wild that she could no longer walk. She stumbled to the stony ledge where she had thrown the fish and bludgeoned one with a stone, then she bludgeoned the other. As she finished striking the second fish, she glanced at her naked self, bared to the air for the first time in more than a year since she had taken her last hot bath in the small room beside the kitchen, in the mistress's old house in the city, and was appalled at how sharp the bones stuck through her skin, as if they were eager to press themselves out. She could trace her ribs, hip bones, the joints of her knees and hips, the long stretch of femurs, the elbow sockets so large in her wasted arms that they seemed as though planted there from a stouter woman's frame. And her skin she saw now was covered in a thick strange hair, perhaps to warm herself, for she had no fat upon her.

She was too full to eat these fish now, so she built a separate fire for them, and made around it a little tent of one coverlet, and set the fillets on a platform of sticks inside to smoke them, to keep them with her in her sack without their rotting to slime. Once more she forced herself to go into the rapids, and she smoked what she did not eat. By the day's end, her belly was so large with fish that it unbalanced her, and her sack had a few days' worth of food in it.

But she had made herself so cold in her greed that she could not whiten her extremities from their purple color though she rubbed at them and put them as close to the fire as she dared without burning herself. The cold had stripped her strength from her. She rose only to creep to a tree and crouch for hot liquid shits, for her sleeping guts had awakened yet again. Then she could hardly bring herself to make a bed of moss and curl upon it between her fires, the one for warming and the one for smoking, and she slept full and deep even though she was out in the open upon the riverbank.

But the next morning, she felt far better, now able to stand freely. Her feet had been bared, warmed by the fire, and the wounds had tightened and stopped their bleeding.

She opened her eyes and lay in her comfort for some time. She saw the redbirds that flicked through the sun and shadow of the woods. She saw the way the tiny translucent green leaves just emerging changed the quality of light as it filtered to the forest floor, so that it seemed to be seething there, strangely golden red.

She wondered why the forest was so clear now, why she could see the beautiful rise of old trees all the way up and down the hills, and why there was no bramble or brush to grab at her and tear holes in her clothing. But she could not find an answer.

For nothing in her ken would allow her to imagine that it was the piscataway, the people of these parts, who so carefully burned the small brush away, and the saplings, too, to better see their game through the trees. She did not know that many of the trees around her were hickory and chestnut and hazelnut and walnut, and that, should she dig below the leaf-litter, she would find ample nuts to sustain her even in these hungry times after the winter and before the full bursting-forth of spring. And that these trees, too, had been planted by the gardeners of this place. For her understanding of gardeners was limited to the ones of the city, and the ones of the city loved a straight line and a neat border, and looking out upon the trees seeming scattered there by the hand of nature itself, she did not recognize the human genius and planning in the wild abundance.

Still, she thought of how familiar she had become with the wilderness she was passing through, and felt pride in herself, for what she once understood about nature now made her laugh aloud. The birds silenced themselves in the wake of this rasping noise. In the city where she was born, she had only known nature on hot and miserable walks on the heath near the river, picking wildflowers and gathering burdocks in her hem that she plucked out later and threw into the fire. She had been on the heath to accompany the mistress who, after the goldsmith's death, sometimes met her gentlemen friends in a secluded place in a silvery copse of trees. For the girl she had been then, all nature was city nature: the mice that scattered and ran whenever anyone opened the pantry door, or the filthy river when it was so low, for the summer was so hot that the vast sturgeon came and lay their bodies upon the face of the water so that they could breathe, and she watched six young apprentices on the bank as they took off their shoes and their hose, and naked-footed waded into the water to lift one of the enormous fish between them and carry it, like pallbearers carrying the dead, out of the shallows.

She had known nothing at all of the natural world when she was raised in the city and yet felt herself very wise in its ways. And now, after having faced it in all her extremity, and after having learned so much, she sensed how deep her ignorance ran and felt dizzy by all that remained to be learned.

A fine drizzle set upon the world and she moved herself under the protection of an oak until it passed. She watched the leaves holding drops that themselves held tiny suns within them. A sense of stillness and light filled her. Within her, all the constant noise hushed. She made herself small. The feeling seemed to pour out of her. The warmth of her body dried her clothes.

The drizzle passed and she walked some more, and as she walked, she found the smooth-barked trees with the tastiest buds and she named these trees Silvers. So naming them, she was suddenly able to pluck them out with her eye from the mass of other trees.

Naming, she understood, made things more visible.

As she walked, she began to name all the things she loved. This early leafless white flower rising on its elegant stalk she called a Maiden-neck, this black-and-white bird that so savagely dove out of its nest at her head when she passed was a Virago bird, this black fly with the red eyes that bit what flesh she exposed to the air was called a Hellspeck. And it was exhilarating to name such things; it was a kind of power. She grew drunk upon it and giddily named everything she saw.

She felt she understood now the first man Adam, how with each name he felt himself growing more powerful, closer to the god who had created and named him. Name after name, Adam felt his dominion tipping into domination until he believed that he owned the world by naming the things in it and that all the things of the world were his to do with as he wished.

For this was how adults granted power to themselves over babies, and how babies without understanding surrendered themselves to adults until they were old enough to name others. How, in coming to this country, her fellow englishmen believed they were naming this place and this people for the first time, and how it conferred upon them dominion here in this place, although, she was now surprised at her thought, surely the people of this place had their own names for things. But one name takes precedence over another, and so the wheel of power turned.

There were only a few who refused to step out of this game. The child Bess, for one, for not only had she been brainless, she had in the end deliberately chosen not to engage, had chosen to let herself die instead of being part of the machinery of domination.

And the child Bess returned to the girl powerfully, chasing with her hand a wag of summerlight through the window, laughing her guttural laugh.

And the mistress saying in a strange moment of gravity, In her very form, my daughter makes real the abstraction of holy grace.

And the child Bess with her soured-milk smell, her apple smell, her faint urine smell because she dribbled over the chamberpot and often pissed on her petticoats and slippers.

And the way that when the girl's own night terrors filled her dreams, sometimes the child Bess's hand was what woke her, patting her cheeks neck hands hair, murmuring wordless comfort until the girl woke fully and chased away her terror.

O put the memory away, girl, she told herself sternly. For the sorrow could eat you entire.

She thought sadly of all her own many names, none of them had ever felt fully hers: Lamentations Callat, Girl, Wench, Zed. The glassblower had called her something in his language, something like Mineheleafda, and this seemed to touch closest to who she was.

But he was dead and trailing silently along behind her. Lamentations Callat was an insult, not a name; Zed, too, an insult and one who had died back in the fort in the starving time.

She would give herself a new name born of her struggle on this new land. It felt wrong for her to travel through this wilderness without a name; she felt she was walking through the world unskinned.

But no name that came to her seemed right, and soon the fever and the walking burned the idea out of her mind, and she went on walking, still nameless, unmastered, through the wilds.

16.

She would be sorry to stop her body's forward motion, for she knew that all the pain would return as soon as she did, that the fever that was now in embers at the base of her spine would flare through her body, so she pressed up a long jagged incline and came out on a ridge with the river rushing whitely down the foot of the cliff upon her right.

At the left hand, a long broad plain unfolded itself unto the horizon.

She gasped in delight and imagined that she could see the entire way across the land and decided that the shimmering blue beyond where her eyes could see must be the other side of the continent, the great and nearly infinite ocean that touched places she had heard of called india and manila, which gave to the apothecaries in the city back home their precious spices.

Could it be, she asked herself, that this new continent was so narrow as this? For if so, how thin the land was, and the ocean did not seem so far from where she stood. It looked to be a flat crossing with no mountains between her and the blue line of sea.

And then she had a vision of herself using perhaps a double of this fortnight or thereabouts that she had been wandering alone in the wilderness to turn westward, to wend her way across the remainder of the land. It would not take her very long. She would dip her feet in the ocean there and see the other coast of the new world.

Glory pulsed in her gut; she, a nobody, a nothing, going farther than any man of europe had yet gone in this place so new to their eyes.

But once there, what else was there to do, who would be there to save her and bring her home again? If none of her countrymen had ever claimed to cross that ocean, none of her countrymen would ever find her. And she would languish alone with her feet in the distant ocean and know she would be alone until she died.

She allowed herself time to stop to rest, to look out upon what she believed to be the end of the continent, to remove her boots and allow the sore and bleeding spots on her feet to cool off in the wind.

The nail in the boot had at last worked all the way through the heel, through the various waddings and paddings, and was now biting into her flesh with every step. But her body was numb in the low boiling fever, and she was glad she did not feel her body fully.

As she sat, she felt her fever settling itself at the base of her neck and pulsing there.

Not far down the western slope of the rise on which she was sitting, at the very base of the trees, were large brown boulders that her eyes played over.

And then one of the boulders suddenly moved. She stared hard. And now she saw that they were not boulders at all, but a strange and cowlike beast with skinny legs and all of their weight bunched up above their shoulders in their heads and necks. One push on the withers, she thought, would send them somersaulting hips over head across the grass.

There were so many of them, dozens or hundreds, all across the valley, farther than her eye could see; she knew from the scale of the trees down in the valley below that these beasts were enormous, that a single one of them would be the double of her own height.

If she were to stand in the middle of them, she would feel overwhelmed with her own smallness and would fear that they would trample her.

O that this place could hold such lovable monsters in it!

She felt a warmth come over her for the land, as hard and unforgiving and wild as it was.

With her knife, she cut two long strips from the coverlet that she had cut into already and wrapped them all around both feet before putting the battered boots back on. The relief of walking with this new padding was great, and she let her legs go faster than they had gone in the morning. She went so fast that her blood beat in her and she nearly panted with the effort.

She came to a narrow space on the trail and looked down to see the rapids only inches beyond her feet, and a stone she had kicked went skittering down the rock face and was lost in the white waters. How easily, too, she could tumble down. But as she stared at the white churning, a bad sense fell over her, a feeling that there was something in the trees behind her, something that was following her.

She looked around wildly and saw a motion that was not the wind in the trees. It was a thing animal. It was a thing large and animal. It was a thing so fast to hide itself that she did not catch a glimpse in full.

And she felt whatever it was watching her from behind a tree.

She turned. She ran. She ran faster and nearly cried out with the pain in her head and could feel behind her that the animal thing that was following her had begun to run behind her and was running faster also.

The path narrowed and she dropped her staff of driftwood down the face of the cliff and it spun on the water and was no longer her own good tool, beloved of her hand, but returned again to the flotsam it had been.

There was a spray in the air and a loudness that she could not stop to understand.

She saw a thin path downward to the river below and took it, scrabbling down with handfuls of grass and the roots of trees to the rocks that stood beside the churning water.

Just days earlier, this river would have been much fatter and swifter with snowmelt and there would have been no place to walk, but now the river had receded, leaving branches from trees along the floodline. She picked her way among them, flying, leaping, as quickly as she could.

She came around a bend to see a vast astonishing waterfall tumbling in five shining sections down five separate high rocky faces. The leftmost, closest to her, was strongest in its high cup of stone, and at its foot was a pool of water churning and flattening outward to a wide blue calm place where she was. Toward the cascade there was a curl of rock barely passable.

Only in her fright would she attempt to take such a slick and difficult path, but she was driven forward and scrambled around the rock, climbing sideways where possible, her gowns already wet through from the moisture in the air and catching at her legs. Nearest the waterfall, there was vivid green foliage, bobbing ferns and grasses where all else in the world beyond was still sending its tender shoots into the spring.

She felt that what was following her was coming yet closer, though she had flown so fast, and she ran through the shallows, and her boots grew wet and the cliff at her side was too high to climb.

In her panicked searching, she saw a ledge at the height of her head disappearing behind the curtain of water. And somehow she scrambled her body up it, shuffled sideways, clinging with her fingertips and inserting her body behind the first of the wild white cascades.

There she would have stayed, clinging, as hidden as possible under the water's roar, should she not have felt the clammy air, then twisted her head low and down inside to see the blackness within the strange invisible hole in the rock face near to hand. With the last of the strength in her, she pulled her body into it. The hole was barely large enough for her body and she lay upon the sack at her waist. She was curtained from sight by the falling water at an arm's length beyond her, though it was laced with open space here and there to see through. The darkness of the little cave held her.

———

She lay shaking with terror in the stone hollow, pressed as far back as she could go with her knees bent, only her head at the lip of it, and she pulled her hood down to darken what gleam there may have been of sweat or tooth or eye, or what else might give her away.

And while she was still panting, only moments after having laid herself down, she saw through the water and the weave of her cloak's hood a man, an actual human man, coming at a run, lightly, around the curve of rock where she had just been.

And he was followed by another man not unlike the first, with a bow taller than he was in his hand and arrows in a woven cone at his waist.

And she was chilled to her soul, for it was reflexive, for she feared the fate of women anywhere, women caught alone on a dark street in a city, in a country lane far from human ears, in any place where there were no other people nearby to witness.

And these new men were both like and unlike the powhatan that surrounded the fort, and she did not know they were of another people that her own people called the piscataway. Perhaps they were still powhatan, she thought, and marveled to imagine how far the reach of their regent would be if that were the case, even in a place like this without horses or metal weapons or gunpowder to enforce dominion.

These men had also insulated their bodies with a thickness of paint against the cold and shaved their long hair on one side so as not to impede the drawing of the bow. And the other hair was held in bands to keep it off their faces. They wore tunics and looked to her otherwise somewhat larger than the men she had grown up among, more powerful in their muscles because, it had been said in the fort by the envious men there, they had had more frequent exposure to meat. And surely their teeth were not the blackened haphazard nubs of her countrymen, either, for which she had heard tell that the sweets of england were to blame.

The men came near so close that she held her breath and did not move, and they pulled themselves up where she had pulled herself up to examine the ledge but did not see the hole where she was hiding. And when they had removed themselves some feet beyond the waterfall and looked all about them, she kept herself still some more and felt herself entirely invisible.

The noise of the falling water was so deafening that she could not hear the men's voices.

At last, they must have decided that in her fear she had leapt into the water and somehow passed them down its churn when they were not looking, because they returned to the pool and one stood staring at the water there, and the other ran back around the way they'd come.

The man who'd remained at the pool crouched low to watch the water and ate something out of the leather sack at his side.

Watching him eat brought up in a terrible nauseating wave all the hunger in her, but she dared not move and give herself away and was glad of the noise of the water for drowning out the noises of her stomach.

Her breath calmed, and she shivered with the chill dampness of her clothing and with the cold in the rocks all around her that pressed into her bones. She watched the man by the pool until the other man returned and the two spoke.

Both men stood and returned the way they had come.

Still, long after they were gone, she could feel them watching from some higher hidden place and she did not dare to move.

But the rock pressing into her had taken on some of her body's warmth and it no longer felt so cold. Her body was still surging with fear, but her brain was somehow lulled by the same fear, and the feeling of being held by the rock and the roar of the water together hushed her to a strange sleep.

In her dreams, she wandered in a darkness so thick that she could not see her hands, she could only feel the path beneath her bare feet, and with each step she took, she feared the next would be over an open drop, and she could feel both the fear of dropping and the drop itself though never the crack against the ground.

When she awakened, the sun was setting in a glory of gold. It reflected upon the still pool beyond the white churn where the water touched in falling. The sharpness of this last light dazzled her eyes.

At her temples, her fever pulsed with her heartbeat, made her jaw ache.

She sensed that perhaps the men were still lingering near, so she would not stir from where she lay, though her whole lower body had gone numb.

She did work her hand slowly under her gown to where the sack was tied to her waist and, one-handed, untied it, and reached in and grasped some smoked fish and brought it to her mouth.

To drink, she understood that she must content herself to open her mouth and catch what spray hit her face and dribbled downward. She ate and she drank and truly she was rather comfortable in this little place that was warm enough and large enough and hidden. The bones of her head did not scream out as she jostled them. And her fever burrowed into her and made her warm. This was not the most wretched she had been, she told herself, and the telling brought still more comfort.

Then the light of the sunset flared out and darkness poured in.

With the thickness of dark now, she did dare move a bit more and she wriggled about to untie the sack from her waist and fold the coverlets under her to keep the cold stone from chilling her body, and she took off her wet boots and the stockings that she could take off and buried her poor wounded cold feet into the delicious warm edge of the coverlet. They looked like dead things, blackened and swollen and ragged, nails gone, smallest toes useless and seeming ready to fall off, wounds thick and bleeding blood and yellow pus. When they had warmed enough, she would put them in the air, she told herself, for the air would cure them, she hoped; but before long, she had fallen back to sleep and she did not.

But in the night, a sense that all was not right awakened her, and she looked through the curtain of falling water for a long while until she could make out what had disturbed her. There at the bend in the little pool was a bear sitting in the shallows, letting the cold water pour over its legs.

It was a giant of a bear. Of all the bears she had seen from afar in this country, this one was far larger, the height of three men standing upon each other's shoulders. And as soon as she could see the bear, she saw the details of it, how the bear's fur gleamed lush in the starlight; and when the moon emerged and shone its brightness upon the pool, she could pick out the details of the bear's face. The beast was looking at the split of the water falling in its five plaits downward. The beast seemed to be paying close attention.

And though she found it hard to read the expression upon a bear's face, she believed that what she saw there was a sense of wonder.

Something within her went out toward the bear in a powerful ripple of sympathy.

There were times when she, also, found herself within a similar up-welling of awe.

Once, in the cathedral in the city, when the mistress, newly widowed of the goldsmith, took the household to hear the new minister preach-ing, she had sat in the pew and watched as the man shone; he was as hand-some as a girl, he looked like a feasted cat, his words were so golden and so sweet that they made all the girls' knees tremble to hear them. At the time, even the girl's own knees had gone soft, for he was seeming hon-eyed inside and out, and she did not know the extent of his badness then.

His words made the mistress's mouth set firm as she looked upon him, and the girl knew her mistress so thoroughly that she could almost see dancing through her mistress's head the tricks and devices she would use to tempt the minister to visit her, to fall within her grasp, to make him her own, though bad he would later prove in this role.

But in the middle of this first and inspired sermon, the girl had looked up to see the light pouring in through the window in such a way that it insinuated itself under the whitewash that covered the popish painting of the saints upon the wall, so that the saints themselves seemed to have stepped out of the whiteness and were looking directly down upon her, insignificant as she was, a mere flea to them, and their faces were glowing with such sorrow, such radiant love, that a godly feeling rushed over her skin, first, then deeper into the meat inside.

And she swooned and would have lost her senses if only she had not pinched her own leg through the fine stuff of her dress until the pain sharpened her and let her stay within the enormous tender glow.

And another time that was not in church she had felt a similar awe, the moment when the lines were cast off and the boat pulled out from the yellow fog of her city in that brave flotilla that pressed toward the un-written world, and she had watched the houses and bridge grow small, smaller, until she was astonished that all she had known, everything that had loomed so large and so important in her days, could easily prove itself such a speck. And it was as though a hand had reached through her ribs and clutched her heart and given it a squeeze.

Now, watching the bear staring upon the waterfall, she felt in her own body the awe that was now coursing through the bear, and within her-self she also felt a shifting in her understanding of the world.

For, if a bear could feel awe, then a bear could certainly know god.

And if a bear could know god in his own bear way, then a bear had a soul, and she could not see how it was that man could feel it was in his right to slaughter such beasts, for in slaughtering the bear's body, man was also slaughtering the beast's soul, which also yearned toward god.

————

And she began to see now that when god created man and woman together and said to let them have dominion over the fish of the sea, and over the fowl of the air, and over the cattle, and over all the earth, and over every creeping thing that creepeth upon the earth, perhaps by dominion god did not mean the right to kill or suppress the fish, the fowl, the cattle, and every creeping thing.

Then she thought that perhaps in the language of the bears there was a kind of gospel, also. And perhaps this gospel said to the bears the same thing about god giving bears dominion over the world. And perhaps bears believed that this gave them license to slaughter the living world, including the men within it.

And this thought made her shake, for if the gospel was changeable between species, then god was not immoveable. Then god was changeable according to the body god spoke through.

And that god could change according to the person in the moment the soul was encountering god.

And this meant that when the godliest of the ministers in the city and in this awful place, back in the fort, spoke on god's behalf they were only speaking a mote of the far greater truth.

They were only speaking the part of god that they themselves could glimpse.

And this truth was only as small as they themselves were small.

————

And perhaps, she thought, god was neither trinity nor singular but mul-
tiple, as various as the many living things that did live upon the earth.

Perhaps god is all.

Perhaps god already lived within all.

And this place and these people here did not need the english to
bring god to them.

The voice that had once in a while chimed into her ear said, very gently,
And what if, girl, god is all; does that mean that, within the all that god
is, there is nothing?

I do not understand, the girl said, and she did not know why but
she was weeping; hot tears were dripping down her skin.

Yes, the voice said, and then was gone.

And the girl listened to the pinprick of light she had carried within her
heart, which she felt all this time was god.

And it was there in the hovel, as she gazed upon the gazing bear,
that nothing replied to her, and nothing echoed back.

She watched the bear and the bear watched the waterfall and the moon
in its elegant thinness watched everything there was upon the earth
below it.

She felt desolate inside, desolate and alone. She summoned the ghost
of her glassblower back to her and imagined him lying in the tight space

alongside her and closed her eyes; and her imagining was so strong that it was as though she were lying in a circle of his arms.

When next she woke, the bear was gone.

The daylight was kindling in the east.

She moved her feet in their beds in the coverlets and her limbs exploded with thousands of tiny bites as the blood rushed back to them, as her blood returned them from the small death of sleep to the pain of waking life.

17.

She sent out her mind and all her attention, and tried to feel all the environs for hint of the men, for perhaps they had stayed the night in vigil.

But she could not sense them near. She believed this meant that they were gone.

Still, with her were two strong presences: the ghost of her glass-blower nearly material if invisible beside her, and the fever, which was burning so hot that the visible world shimmered at its edges and her underdresses were soaked in sweat.

She sat herself upright. She ate more of the smoked fish and reached out the pewter cup to catch the water cascading in a curtain before her and drank deeply. In experiment, she licked the water off the wall of the cavern, and it tasted of salt.

Then she packed her things away in the sack and tied it about herself again.

For some time, she thought of putting on the boots, but if in climbing down the rock face she slipped and fell into the water, she was afraid that the boots would drag her to the bottom of the pool. And so she tied the latchets together and hung the boots around her neck, then lowered herself with her arms and searched for the crack in the stone with her bare toes.

At last, she found it when her arms had nearly given out. She edged to the fuller ledge then down to the slick stones that rimmed the pool.

The water on her feet was shocking cold, but as her fever boiled her blood hot, the mist cooled her face and felt like a fine soft silk upon her skin.

She found her way to the top of the cliff face and put her wrappers on her wounded bleeding feet, then laced her boots on again. The dried leather groaned in protest.

Without building a fire to warm herself, she returned to the woods, where there was more opportunity to hide if she had any need of hiding.

She would leave this place as soon as she could; she would put as much land as it was possible to put between herself and the men or the bear; she did not know which to fear more, man or bear or perhaps her own small starved feverish self.

And so, though the ache in her feet was mighty, she made her steps fleet until she felt herself running.

She had heard—where was this?—yes, held fast upon Kit's knee when she was very young as he translated from the latin into english tales of women who had run away and, in running, had become other things. A beautiful maiden, ravished and punished for the violation by becoming a white heifer that leapt a river. Girl become sunflower. Girl become dove. Girl become raven. Girls, all the many girls fleeing from pursuers, girls who were turned, even in their flight, into trees.

And she ran as fast as her legs could take her, ran until all her breath was lost; and she did not have the force to step over a tree root fully, and tripped upon it, and fell from the path and tumbled down into a gap full of wintry dry leaves. There, as she lay, all her power left her. If her followers had loomed above the rise, whether they were real or imagined, she could not have stood to run anew.

And it was there, lying in the gap of leaves, that she felt herself turning into a tree.

And it was as if in vision that she heard the command whispered by the wind and saw the open hole in the tree luring her in, the headlong dive, the hole closing from all sides into blackness, and the hunters' footsteps unheard but thundering past in vibration through the woods. Then the glorious growing, her feet stretching down to burrow luxurious into the rich loam of the forest, taking root, the crown rising above the trees, the arms outstretching multiply, arms growing arms, fingers bursting to leaf, and yearning toward the sun.

Her heartbeats, as she lay, diminished from a gallop to a trot. And the noise of the forest returned to her.

She closed her eyes and the ghost of the glassblower stood before her holding his hand out, urging her on.

She stood and groaned with the pain despite her need for silence.

And though her lungs burned hot in her chest and her broken head pulsed and her joints and feet screamed, she ran again. And after some time running, the running became sweet to her, the pain silenced itself, and she no longer felt her body at all, only the goodness of the run.

She stopped when in a bush she saw a flash of bloodred, and she took a dried berry off a bush and ate it. And it was good, though so sour that it numbed her tongue in going down, and she threw fistfuls of the berries into the sack and ate another handful. And, so fortified, she ran on.

The sun grew strong in midday, and though the wind was cold, she felt herself so hot that she took off the cloak and shoved it in the sack. Later, when she was still sweating, she took off two of her gowns as well and ran in her thinnest gown closest to her skin, which was soaked with sweat and so verminous and filthy that the smell offended even her own nose and the sight of the hems crawling with lice offended her eyes.

And soon she was too hot even for this last gown.

And feeling herself so wondrous solitary in the wilderness, and her brains made sluggish by the fever, she believed she had left her pursuers far behind her. So she untied the sleeves of this gown, which were blackened with armpit stink and the long year of sweat and sickness. And she shoved the sleeves into the sack and allowed the skin of her arms to be bared to the sun.

And this feeling of sun upon her was delicious and good.

The sun upon her was a benediction.

She was running now on a ridge that rose along the land like a spine, and in her fever, she saw the land as the back of a vast creature curled into the rock and sleeping.

———

Then voices began to filter down to her, coming out of her memory, speaking out of the dazzling sun of this place. And they were the voices of the players and poets who had filled her days as a child in the mistress's sitting room when she was a singing dancing fool. Endless gossip these voices spoke, and joke, and insinuation. The meaty-headed poet with the red beard, his friend who designed the poet's masques and sketched the girl one day on the margin of a musical score, in the form of a smiling spinning top. These men's mutual friend and enemy, a sparrowlike man with a gold earring who jostled his legs with too much energy and scribbled things that had been said in a tiny book with a clever whittled piece of lead. As well as, of course, the little lordling with the face and hair of an angel with whom everyone was in love or at least pretended to be.

And in the middle of it all, the mistress laughing, the mistress these clever men's own queen, who collected their love poems as taxes for her attention and her claret.

Ah, Tiny Mischief, the red and fleshy poet was calling the girl invisibly all the way distant here in the wilds the way he had once called her Tiny Mischief in the city. Tiny Mischief, come now, sit on my lap, I'll not hurt thee.

And in her mouth, she tasted both a spice cake and the fat finger that pushed it in.

Tiny Mischiefs, like beasts, do feed until they're fat, he said in her ear, goosing her.

And then they bleed, the sparrowlike poet said drily, watching with his sharp eyes.

———

By afternoon, having long been sunk in her visions, she looked up. She stopped.

She had nearly run into a place so strange that she at first believed it to be an emanation of her fever. It was a small pool ringed by pale birch trees that leaned their crowns together, touching. Yet in this newly awakening forest with its bare buds, the leaves of these trees were full and green, and cast upon the place a filtering shimmering light. From the top of the water, plumes of steam rose and played at tag in the wind that whispered and circled here.

She bent to the water and touched it with her hand and found it as hot as a bath.

She looked all around her but saw only the forest, still and bright, looking back at her.

So she took off her last gown, her boots, the wrappings, her hose, the stockings ripped unto lace.

She took off her stinking undergarments.

Naked in the full light of day, she walked into the hot pool. She dipped her body under the water and held her breath, and when she came up, it was in a black slick of filth and oil and lice and fleas off her body, which made rings upon the surface of the water.

It was so warm that the day spun in her eyes.

She that is giddy thinks the world turned round, a voice said in her ear, quite loud.

She pushed with her arms until the circles of filth rippled away, and went under again and held her breath for as long as her lungs could stand.

And when she came up this time, the new upwelling of filth and bugs was only brown, not black, and there were fewer insects in it.

She floated upon her back in the glorious heat. She felt the curls of mist drift and jostle over the small skin exposed in the air.

Her long hair loosed itself from the knot she had tied it into, then loosed were the many plaits that made up the knot.

Her wounds smarted in the heat.

She felt the sharpness of her bones going soft.

She sank her clothing under the water with a stone so that the insects came floating up drowned in an endless stream of filth.

She considered, then took the sack and emptied it and gathered up all the fabric and sank it also to drown the beasties within.

After she had wrung out the fabric of her good coverlets, the sack, and the clothing, and hung them upon the branches of trees to dry in the sunlight, she plucked the nits away from her groin and her armpits one by one and drowned them in the water. She scraped the nits from her scalp and crushed the lice and the fleas under her fingernails until she could find no more.

And all this took many hours, nearly the full afternoon, and her flesh was exposed to the water so long that she first became fat with water then wrinkled with it.

She stood, hearing through the sounds of the busy forest a low humming noise as though something were singing to itself out of a throat of wood.

She came naked over the muddy ground toward the sound that

seeming trembled her bones as she neared it. In one of the oaks that ringed the birches, like a strong sentry protecting slender pale tender maidens, she found a hole at the height of her head. When she peered inside the hole, she saw the black and yellow stripes of hundreds or thousands of humble-bees, with their rears shivering outward to make warmth for their hive.

And she did not stop to reflect but plunged her hand through the slumbering bees and felt her fingers and palm go into a deeper warmth and softness.

And when she pulled her hand out again, it was covered in golden honey, with struggling bees stinging all over her flesh and flecks of comb like fine crumbs of bread upon it. She licked the honey full off her hand and plunged it in again and again, not caring about the stings.

She ate until her blood sang with sugar and her hand and arm were so swollen with stings that she could not bend them, until the bees were too angry for her to risk any more. Then she ran again into the water and went under and held her breath and watched from below as above the surface the bees darted and searched to punish her. She came up only for a breath and went down again. Again and again, she came up only to breathe, and soon, her enemies being only bees, they forgot her and returned to busily fixing what she had broken of their hive.

She climbed out again and with a long stick this time poked into the hive and fled to escape the wrath of the bees. With the honey off this stick, she painted the bright fresh wounds of her feet and legs. For, she remembered, in the city, the cook had used honey against burns and wounds and the bruises that rose to the surface of the skin when Kit had hit the girl in the face. And it had felt to her that the healing had been as magic. A salve of sweetness. She gasped at the sting of the honey upon the wounds. In the late sunlight, she let it dry upon her naked body.

And she stood, clean and warm in this strange place, and gave thanks to the humble-bees for their blessing of honey.

She dressed, languid from the heat of the water and the long run of the day. Her clothes, though much cleaner and dry from the sun now, still held a stink that was new to her, as her own stink of her body that had masked the clothing's odors had been washed away.

The sack with her things in it felt newly cumbersome. Her wet hair, although she had braided it again and twisted the braids up into a knot, felt so heavy that it dragged her throbbing head back. Fatigue had settled in her bones.

Still, she walked on, for she had lost all other idea of what else to do than go forward.

In her walking, the honey she had eaten filled her brain with vivid daydreams.

She discovered herself in the city of her birth again, and, as during the terrible summer of the most recent plague when the bells rang and never ceased ringing in the grief for the departed, there were bells now ringing alarm and death constant into the air. The dogs, she knew that bad summer, had been caught and drowned, for it had been thought the disease was spread by curs, but it was not curs, for after the slaughter of the street dogs, the disease kept up its own relentless slaughter. In the beds of the houses, the bodies were stacked like firewood. Royalty in their towers above the miasma of sick were still infected and, coughing, fell. Paupers died in their rags in the dozens beneath the bridge. Vicars scuttled in panic with masks upon their faces and incense from the stores of the papists to burn off infection, and even the sternest godliest of these men died like so many bugs.

And the old goldsmith, the mistress's first husband, tottered home sweating, all the household fleeing from his path, the mistress shouting down the stairs to where he had come staggering into the entryway, O husband, I commend thy soul to god.

And she barred him with the bodies of the gardener and the stable boys from coming up the stairs to his own apartments.

Then she ordered the sign nailed upon the front door and the windows to be boarded lightless for six weeks, and she had the cook, who would sleep in the stables, venture into the sick city to purchase food and raise a bucket up for meals for the mistress and the child Bess and Kit who was home from the university, for the university was also sick.

When the girl tried to climb the stairs to be with the child Bess and the rest, the cook, in the mistress's absence, cried out, Ah, nay, pathetical nit, it is thou who must tend to the old master, for only thou of the household hast nursed the plague-sick in that cesspit rathole of a poorhouse that they pulled thee out of.

True, the girl tried to say, that she had nursed those poor babes in the poorhouse who died one by one in her childish skinny arms, but not a single babe had survived her care.

But the cook ignored her protests and others that she raised, that she was but still a girl and that it was improper for a maiden to be closed in a room with a grown man; and having stopped up her ears, the cook thrust the girl bodily inside the downstairs chamber with the shaking quaking master, the welts already rising black from beneath his skin. Then the servants put in a tray of black bread and a pitcher of beer and armfuls of firewood and a trundle of aquavitae and rags for the girl to bathe his body with.

And behind her, they nailed the door shut, leaving her in the black with the quavering man.

But for how long? the girl cried out. Answer me, you mad-brain rudesby of a trull.

Thou base minnow, shallow vessel, the cook bellowed back. Stay until the master dies or he dies not; it is no matter of mine.

May you drown in a malmsey butt, welsh hag, the girl said. Tell me how long that might be.

She had no answer, for there was no one beyond to answer, for all the servants had fled the sick house for the stables. She tried not to weep. She pressed her face against the cool wood of the door.

I believe, said the goldsmith in his gentle voice, it will be no longer than four days and perchance less.

The girl turned toward him in the bleak terror of the chamber, all dark save for the sunlight shining in the small high window, illuminating his pink crown and around it the ring of fine white hair.

The goldsmith was lying on the cot and weeping weakly.

O almighty god, the girl said, which in thy wrath in the time of King David didst slay with the plague of pestilence threescore and ten thousand, and yet remembering thy mercy didst save the rest, have pity upon us miserable sinners that now are visited with sickness and mortality. That like as thou didst then command thine angel to cease from punishing, so may it now please thee to withdraw from us this grievous sickness. Amen.

Then she made the fire large and bright, for though it was hot summer outside, the light was necessary to keep the frantic visions of death from stealing over the master's brain. Or else, she feared, she would be closed into a chamber with a madman.

The poor master's hands were quaking so deeply now that he could not undress himself. She was moved to pity and came near and helped him. How thin and pale he was, set into his linens. She felt an anguish to see him so reduced.

Read to me, child, he said. O do not say that you cannot read. Could it be that my wife, who does love books so true, has not taught you? A sin, this, to keep a girl as bright as you from her letters. If I should live beyond my sickness, I shall teach you. Well, there will be no books now, as my eyes do not seem to be working as they ought. We shall pass the time by telling stories.

So she told him all the stories that teemed in her brain from hearing the talk of the mistress's friends: the fiendish fairies in the palaces under the hill and the human child they stole and left a clay creature in its stead. The princess with the shoes that made her dance until she died. The dragon who ate all the cows of the fields until a wise farmer made a ginger pudding with poison in it and pretended it was an offering for protection, and the dragon did gobble it up, and the clever farmer saved all the land and was made king for his wisdom.

She ran out of stories when the church bells rang their midnight song and sleepiness began to steal over her.

I am sorry, master, I have no more to tell, she said.

By now, the master was panting, for he had begun drowning in his lungs.

A fine storyteller you are, child, he said.

But he was unable to bear the silence and began to tell his own tales, gasping and wheezing between words. Himself a mere boy running from the farm with its hated pigs, walking down from scotland with dry bread and a farthing and a furious spirit, making his way in the city with vice at first, but becoming an apprentice in the blue hose and re-penting, coming to god. And later, through hard work, he became a rich man, a goldsmith master, and after a lifetime and late marriage to the mistress, he, who began an unlettered scottish lad, had nearly been elected lord mayor, and twice.

It took him very long to tell this story, but she had nought else to do but listen.

And then he said, Child. I am afraid. I am old. But not ready. To die.

O, she said, for she was a fool and could not help it, Well, master, dying is a skill learned only in its undertaking.

Undertaking! he laughed. Then he began to cry.

When the sickness made the goldsmith yet more wild in his fear, he forgot who it was that sat in the shadows with him, and in painful gasps told a story of the man who had lost his male member and the witch he asked for help. Aye, the witch said, Ye can hae a new member, just climb yourself up to my wee nest in the tree and choose which does suit ye best of the many male members my devoted congregation hath given to me. And the man climbed up and chose the largest and fattest member, and brought it down proudly. The witch took one look and said sadly, Nae, but ye cannot hae that one, for it belongs to the archbishop.

The goldsmith laughed until he choked on laughing, then he choked upon his own lungs.

Soon after, he gave a strange and rattling breath then breathed no more, for he was dead.

And his face in the firelight seemed to move all night, for when the girl shouted and screamed, and a groom came to ask angrily what she wanted, he went away and came back presently saying that the viewers of the dead were too drunk to come until morning, and the door would not be unsealed until they came.

She built the fire high and bright, for upon the visage of the dead man there was pressed a stark terror. She found it strange that he would be so terrified, for he had been godly in his life, and the proof was clear that for eternity he would find himself among the elect, for how else would god show his favor but by giving him a rich house, a stout son Kit at the university, a beautiful and musical wife, and a daughter of innocence and gold, as well as the tapestries and furniture and all the many goodnesses and comforts he had had in his life.

And she marveled that, though the soul had entered into this promised eternity and his body was cooling in death, still the master's face in the flickering moved in grimaces of horror.

The girl sat with this vision of hell all the long and endless night and into the day, and could not sleep for terror. Haunted by the death face, for months she quavered and cried in her sleep.

Upon the household there fell a full year of public sobriety after the master's death.

Then the mistress cast off her widow's weeds, and not long after, she listened to the honey-tongued minister and was beguiled. She was nearly ill in the hunger in her flesh for him.

One night after the girl had begun to see the viper coiled within the minister, she was brushing out the mistress's hair when the mistress sighed and said, O but he is fair.

His skin bears a pallor, it is true, the girl said slowly, knowing of whom the mistress spoke.

A pallor! No, but he is fair like the sun that shines its warming rays on all who turn their faces to him, the mistress said.

He does have a too-hot fire within, which, perhaps, burning hot, turns him so white, the girl said.

No, my imp, he is fair on the inside, the mistress said. A tongue cannot speak words so honeyed without a reserve of sweetness within. How tender he is, how much he blushes at a lewd gibe. A window for a man, his blushes show his soul.

As glass is brittle, so is he, the girl said, laying down the brush.

How, brittle? the mistress said, frowning.

With pride too easily broke, and the jagged shards kept to hand to cut another with.

It is your tongue that is too sharp, fool Zed. Sheathe it now, for he shall be mine.

Then own him as a toy, not a yoke, the girl said.

Not a yoke but mayhap a saddle. The mistress laughed. I shall bear his weight and he shall ride, until under him I die and die again.

And after she had so prettily maneuvered her will to life and married the minister swiftly, the noises that came from her chamber did make it seem as though the mistress was being throttled to death, only for her to be reborn by morning. And this, too, appeared to the girl, who had been cast from the chamber where she had slept when the minister came in, to be another kind of horror, not once to die of plague but again and again nightly.

And as she walked fever-dreaming all this memory into life again, something new now struck her with the force of truth.

She stopped to gawk but there was nothing about her but darkening trees.

There had come to her, solid and clear, the understanding in her rattled brains that in the time of her absence from it the known world, her natal city of dirt and noise and pig and horse and overweening life and all the other cities in the entirety of civilization, all the screaming fishwives and all the barristers and musicians and the servants, all had been struck down by the most terrible plague the world had ever seen.

And she felt it, she could feel it, in these distant wastes, that this was a plague that no human bodies could survive.

And this far worse plague of her imagination filled her mind with visions. For all the human noises in her city diminished to silence, the bells stopped pealing, the voices were no more; the only sound was the wind blowing up the miles from the sea, the kites screaming and pecking at the bodies of the dead, the gulls and pigs and dogs out fighting for their scraps, and the collapsing of roofs and shattering of windows without the many hands of humans to keep the city alive.

Wind shredding the curtains of the theaters.

Gray mice running rampant in herds, chewing the precious books held in the libraries of the universities.

The painting of the new king moldering upon the wall, falling out of its frame.

The barns where the cows moaned for the ache of their swollen teats, then one by one they died and became leaning skeletons.

Horses roaming free and vicious, having forgotten what it meant to be mastered.

And in the fields, the trees would take root and in two seasons cover all the countryside where there once had been grains. And in five, they would resemble the virgin woods of these unknown lands. And in ten years, all traces of human habitation in the countries of the world would be grown over with vegetation and the animals gamboling, delighted without the greatest palest predator to stop them.

And Eden would overtake the world and the mistake of man would be forgot.

Perhaps in her innermost heart, she thought, this was no fever-vision but a wish, a wish that they all die, that a mighty hand would come from the heavens to crush them, every last one.

And the voice in her ear said, silky, Dost thou truly hate thine own kind so much, girl?

And the girl looked upon the vast and stretching canopy of the trees, the birds thick flying branch to branch, the sun in softness falling through the new leaves and shivering with happiness upon the ground, and said with sadness, My people would look upon such places and hate what they saw, would replace it all with cobbled streets and smithies throwing black clouds of smoke into the air.

You did not answer me, child, the voice said sternly.

And she thought of the suffering, the death of the children, and said aloud, I do not hate my own people enough to smite them all.

Though in her heart perhaps she said yes.

And when she became aware of the yes in her heart, she began to believe that all of the civilization of her people was gone entirely, that she had brought disaster upon them with her secret wish, and what remained of the greatness of generations of englishmen was only what she held in her fevered brain.

That she, insignificant, a mote in god's eye, had now become the human keeper of all that would otherwise be lost.

She, the least of human beings, the lowest, must now live, to remember, her fever told her.

She must preserve the goodness that had been in that world.

She must give it to the humans of this, newer, world.

The songs, she would recall, the poems, the best of art.

So she sang aloud now into the forest where she had summoned catastrophic plague upon her own kind far across the sea: In spring-time, the only pretty ring time, when birds do sing, hey ding a ding ding, sweet lovers love the spring.

Then the honey burned full out of her and she could no longer move her body. Her hands throbbed with swollenness in concert with her throbbing head.

She stopped for the night.

The warmth of the day had gone and a chill had stolen in with the dark. She put all of her clothing back on again. She ate of the smoked fish until she was full, drank, pissed.

Then she made use of two fallen logs that rose to the level of her waist, so that in that way they formed a crib just larger than her body, and she filled the space between the logs with armfuls of the rasping dried leaves still on the ground from the distant autumn.

She inserted herself into this soft sweet-smelling pile of leaves and let them cover her and warm her as though they were another coverlet. There would be no fire, for she was too tired to coax a fire alive.

In her mouth was a new sore that her tongue could not cease probing.

Well, she reassured herself, it was true that the entirety of her body was an open sore now.

And all around her there were rustlings and chirpings; she was sharing this space with a family of chipmunks or flying squirrels or some other creatures, good mouthfuls if she could catch them, but she did not try.

For something in her after this day loved the comfort of laying her head down peacefully among the small and unseen creatures of the wilderness.

18.

When she woke shivering in the night, her fever searing hot, she knew her leaf crib was not enough, so she rose out of it. She gathered dry branches off the bottoms of the fir trees and built a little fire and made her coverlet tent over half of it so that the heat could be trapped by the wool. This allowed her to stop shivering enough to sleep again.

The day visions had left her and the night visions had set in.

In the worst vision of the night, she looked up in terror and saw a black mountaintop as though she were somewhere near its root. And out of the sky at the top of the mountain, there was a single star falling out of the black. It grew larger and larger then came crashing down, a glowing stone, and she could hear it falling against the mountain, smashing and rolling swiftly down; it sounded like footsteps, it crashed nearer and nearer, it was coming toward her, this ball of fire; and she woke to see a black snout pressing against the stick that held her tent up. Then the stick and the tent collapsed together. The coverlet's edge fell into the fire. The grease in the wool caused it to go up in a roar of flame.

She scrambled backward from underneath the flaming coverlet and hid on the other side of the tree and watched as the single vast male wolf, whose haunches rose to the height of the top of her head, leapt back from the sudden fire, the fur along his spine spiking out and shining terror in his eyes at the sudden spitting green flames.

She had just enough presence of mind to reach around the tree and pull the other coverlet and her sack from where the wolf was, toward herself in her crouch behind the tree.

The wolf could not see her now; in its terror it could only see fire, and she heard it retreat, its steps heavy over the brush and dead leaves of winter. She held her breath and prayed inside her head.

When she felt certain that the wolf was out of range, she crept back, and with all the sticks that she gathered, she built a fire on three sides of herself, with the tree to her back.

Within the fires, she examined the unburnt remainder of coverlet, singed black at its edges.

She wrapped it around her neck as a muffler and tucked the ends into the top of her innermost gown. The stink of charred wool overcame all the other stinks of her person and became a new companion.

She stayed awake until morning, when she had a vision of how she might look to another of her people if he happened out of the woods and discovered her there; she would appear to him a starved and wizened urchin with feverish eyes and a blue-black growth upon her crown like the growing horn of a devil, who was wearing garments of the most wretched rags, worse than any beggar on the streets of a city, a body nearly but not quite dead. She gave a small and bitter laugh.

Then fearful of the horrible teeth of the lonely wolf, each one of which had been as long as her hand, she waited in the circle of fire for daylight. It came falsely a thousand times, but at long last, just as she was despairing, the true sun set itself alight into full blaze at the edge of the sky.

19.

Perhaps it was the shock of the wolf, perhaps the journey had finally weakened her beyond the first weakness of her long starvation, for as the sun rose on her fifteenth day alone in the wilderness, so too the illness that had been her steady companion, the fever she had so long been trying to burn off, rose through her and manifested itself.

Quietly, what bad seeds that had ridden in her blood since the settlement now flowered upon her skin.

She had watched people die of the bilious fluxes, the shitty fluxes, the bloody fluxes, the brackish swellings, the scurvy, the venereal lues, the yaws, the grander pox and the smaller pox, the plague, the fevers both fecal and malarial as well as the tertian and quotidian and pestilent fevers, the consumptions, the swellings of the body from drinking water unboiled and from drinking water too salty, from the surfeit of choler and the surfeit of blood, from the arrows of the men of this place and the rope of the hangman. She had seen thieves tied to trees starve to their death, wretchedly hastened by the bite of cold and hunger that ate them all from the inside out. Worst was when the child Bess died of refusing to live. Second-worst was the time a man, gone mad from the gnawing constancy of his hunger, slaughtered his wife and salted her limbs and hid them in the rafters of his house. The babe within her he did not eat but threw into the river, and thus his murder was discovered. He was caught and hanged by the thumbs in the bitter cold until dead, gone full animal in the face and biting at anyone who stopped by to pray over his blue body and observe his sufferings for their own moral edification.

Not a day passed in the winter of the starving time without a few people dying, and she had seen so much dying that she knew well the symptoms of death.

She checked each part of her body to discover what disease it was she had begun suffering from. There was the sore in her mouth that had grown into many sores there. She had the hot black shits but it was likely the berries she was eating; her lungs ached and there was a wheeze, but she checked her throat and legs and arms and saw no purple buboes.

But when she looked at the bared skin of her arms and legs, she did see a telltale redness there and reached up and felt it in its new soreness around her mouth.

It was the smallpox, then. And this the fine red rash of the early stages.

She thought of the gentleman's son, his wasted body so overrun with pustules that they were between his toes when she pulled the boots off him.

These boots, which had carried her so faithfully these many miles.

She closed her eyes and the glassblower was before her, his face full of sympathy.

But she opened them and laughed, for this was a misery she knew well; she had observed it often; at the mistress's there had been that poor child groom whose body had been disfigured forevermore from his bout with the disease, who survived but hobbled about, for his genitals had been terribly scarred.

The babe at the poorhouse as well, whose face had so been eaten up by pustules that it no longer had eyes or nostrils or lips left, only a hole for a mouth in a thickness of blisters.

She despaired, laughing, and could not stop.

O lord, she said aloud, should I stop my journey here in this place, should I lay myself down in the sun to die?

And she listened to the wind and the trees and the beasts and the birds, and took no answer from them until it was her own voice that rose up harsh and terrible in the day. No, she said aloud. Go on.

Forward she staggered. Her fever was shattering her. It gathered a storm at the center of her neck and in the small of her back.

She rued the driftwood crook she had dropped back at the rapids in flight from the men. She found a replacement stick to help her walk, and it was sturdy enough but had no wit or charm and was not a good companion.

Perhaps if she still moved, she thought, there was yet a chance.

Perhaps she could move as far northward as the french were before the smallpox rendered her immobile; they would let her stay in a stable and place food near her, and her pox would burn out of her and she would heal once more.

Though there was still food in her sack, she could not eat it. She had lost her appetite along with the largest part of her hope when she felt the sores around her mouth and knew she was stricken.

Her footsteps slowed.

Now she shuffled.

Up, up, up an endless hill. She gasped with pain. She rested upon a fallen tree to steady herself.

Into her head floated snatches of song as though someone were singing them nearby, perhaps it was her own voice singing them, and out of her head floated the songs.

She came shuffling into a sunbright copse and stopped in wonderment.

For here in the clearing there was the cook's table as it had been the final Shrove Tuesday before the mistress married the preacher and followed his ambitions into the new world and ruined all their lives.

The table was spread with the tablecloth trimmed in lace, tapers burning lushly in the silver sticks, a suckling pig smiling up at her through a mouthful of apple, his own skin red and crisp and ready to crackle apart with the touch of a fork. A large salmon lay upon a bed of sliced lemons and lettuces, there was a roasted swan with head tucked back, a honeyed trout, a dish of doves, a salat lustrous with oil and ham and candied fruit and olives like an ornament shining in the center of the table, like the diadem glistering on the white stretch of the mistress's painted brow. There were breads and cheese and fruits and meat pies and a flight of pastry birds with startled gooseberry eyes. And at the end of the table there sat the cook's crowning glory, a whole miniature tyburn sculpted entirely of marchpane, complete with nobles and ladies and commonfolk in the audience, with hackney coaches at the wait, with stands full of people to watch the events and tiny nutsellers and the women selling hot codlings and the fortress on the side. The finest work of the cook's hands was in the three cleverly molded thieves already dangling dead on the gibbet tree.

O she was there, she had returned, she could reach out and touch this orange right here and watch its torn flesh spray a fine juice into the air; the sun shone through the windows and lit up the dust in its golden flinging motes, and down on the streets below, the apprentices ran and laughed at the crash of a cart that they were overturning, and above in the air, there was a frenzy of churchbells. Now the sweet child Bess was beside the girl once more, she smelled of piss and milk, she cooed and greedily grabbed at a bowl of figs and sucked at one, slobbering over her hand. The girl once more could reach out and grasp the sweet softness of her heart's dearest love to herself and hold her tight and breathe her own child Bess in until she, tired of being squeezed, batted at her face, laughing, then put her shining head upon the girl's shoulder. The child Bess slipped into the girl's hand some nothing, some stolen thing, a silver spoon the mistress stirred her rosewater with and loved dearly for her own initials engraved upon it. The mistress was playing her lute in the corner and singing low in her throat. And the child Bess looked the girl full in the face, as she did not like to do, and gave a wetlipped smile, and there was an overwhelming richness inside the girl that any words that she could summon would have been too weak and writhled to hold.

The vision faded. Her hand scrabbled at the empty air. The trees were clacking their branches; the trees were laughing down at her.

She walked.

Foot of fire after foot of fire.

Whole body blazing. Alit. Ecstatic.

A step again. A step again.

Into the twilight she walked. Her eyes did close but she moved unseeing.

Outside her a darkness of night fell.

Inside there was a darkness of the nothing of god.

Once, she opened her eyes to a moonlit clearing, the trees hunched at the edges into an ardent watching forest; the spring-stirred soil smelled tender in the silvery night, and thickening the sky with its barest of light was the near-dissolved rim of moon.

Once, she opened her eyes and saw herself slowly moving up a hill. On the ground there were shivering globes where the light crept through branch and leaf. In the globes were brightly shining mushrooms, fist-sized mushrooms painted red and orange and yellow with long elegant white stalks, and mushrooms so like a man's privies immodestly erect that, despite the sorrows of her body, she laughed with astonishment. Then she kicked the mushrooms to pieces.

———————

Once, she opened her eyes to find that she was high on a cliff, hands pressed to stone, sliding foot after foot on a path so narrow that only half her foot could rest upon it and the other half hung into the yawning dark. And this was so surprising to her that she cried out and her body jerked and, in jerking, sent her sliding off one foot, and she groped for the wall but felt only rough grains beneath her fingers and no crack or ledge to hold on to. Then the other foot slipped sideways and her whole foot slipped over and she was falling; she hit her hip hard on the ledge and it scraped up her abdomen, her ribs, her chin, her cheek, her temple, her upstretched arms, and her wrists banged upon the ledge and could not grasp at it, and she was hurtling down now, hurtling through the darkness, and she saw the pocked and pitted face of the cliff being slowly pulled upward before her like a gray curtain. For how long she was falling she did not know. She must have swiveled in the air, for she hit the ground upon her side in a heap of damp dirt and heard within her body a sharp cracking sound, then she slid and slid and came to rest against a boulder velveted to two fists deep with moss. And there she slept.

20.

I t was full day when she woke.

A long green insect was walking before her eyes with mincing steps and preacher's hands.

Birdsong rioted the air.

Breathing hurt on one side.

She moved her fingers; she moved her toes. Hands and feet, arms and legs.

She turned on her back and looked up. The cliff she had fallen from was only as tall from where she was lying as a man on a knee-high stepstool. She had slid down a mossy bank. Not a long fall, then a landing softer than water.

And the moss and the insects and the birds sang her to sleep again.

When she woke, she stood to walk forward once more, and this new suffering, which in the city of her birth would have made her mewl like a babe and take to a cot, was hardly a ripple in all the waves of what she felt.

Go on, go on, go on, girl, she said aloud to herself, angry. Go on or die where you stand.

And so she went, slower still, but at least she was walking.

Shuffling, but her body was so heavy that even shuffling was a triumph.

She came out into an opening at the top of a hill. There was a wheezing squealing music like a bagpipe all around, and the music was coming from her.

From where she was, the land tilted dangerously downward both to the east and the west, and she could see her own good river joined by another river that ran into it from the south. She watched this most intimate moment of joining.

As she stood there looking, thick woolen clouds were being blown down from the north, and they stretched across the whole of the distant sky. She looked at them with pleasure. How lovely they were, how fine and purple. She touched the scorched fragment of coverlet around her neck and thought how she would have preferred the cloud-coverlet above to lie against her skin, how much softer the cloud looked. It seemed as if woven of dark and silken hair. She made hand motions as though pulling it up over her face. She imagined it warm on the skin and blotting out the bright sun where she stood. It was coming swiftly southward toward her, carrying beneath it such a dense black shadow that all the trees and water the shadow fell upon were suddenly darkened to night.

But the fabric of the cloud was being pulled open by the speed of its movement, and now great holes were opening up in it. Through the holes, the dazzling bright sun poked its long pale fingers and touched the ground, and the trees that the light suddenly singled out from the rest appeared so perfect, such pristine exemplars of their species, that she did not know how she did not see each tree's perfect beauty before this moment.

It is a moral failure to miss the profound beauty of the world, said the voice in her mind.

Yes, she said aloud, for now she did see the sin in full.

And even as she looked out upon the black cloud, the blacker shadows upon the earth, the sideways beams of light, and the illuminated trees, she saw that the light was not what she had thought it was. Each beam was a ladder made out of strongest sunlight, and upon the ladders were angels busily moving themselves up and down.

So industrious they were, the angels!

How like shining divine ants they were!

A heat of joy spread through her, radiating outward from her heart into her arms and fingers and legs and toes and even into her sore and blighted skin when her eyes did see all these many busy angels.

It was as a salve to her. It was as a long cool draught after a terrible thirst.

The busy angels were there for her, she understood; they had come for her, and she must hurry to join them.

She cried out, Wait, I arrive! and started to run down the hillside, which was so steep that in places it sheared off into cliff, which she dodged and had to find a new way to descend. But in places the path was straight and steep, and her wobbly half-dead legs could hardly keep up with the speed of her body in its descent, and the sack pulled so heavily on her waist that it caught like a tail between her legs and caused her to stumble.

She looked down to place her feet with more care on a tricky slope and slowed a little.

When she looked up, she saw that the cloud had moved; the rents in the coverlet of cloud had closed, every last one; the coverlet was thick and healed and dark across the whole sky above her.

The ladders had been withdrawn.

The angels were gone.

The angels had left her alone upon this world in her wretchedness and sickness and suffering.

She gave a cry half-animal and was flung to the ground.

All that was good in her fled her, her resolve and hope and faith.

All the goodness fled her.

Into the vacuum poured thick despair and all the many monsters she had locked behind the heavy door in her mind.

The angels were gone; she understood that there had never been any angels.

Light was simply light, unpeopled by hope.

There was a great emptiness, and even the clouds in their thickness were bereft.

The rain was cold and fell in gouts upon her, and she lay upon her back and allowed the wet to drum upon her skin. Her body was quaking as though to break her limbs against the hard ground.

The storm passed soon. She was wet but not wet enough for the wet to kill her. Her sickness was growing but simply not fast enough to kill her. Her hunger was a beast prowling in her, but it had also not yet killed her.

The nothing revealed in her where once had burned the small hot flame of god had not killed her.

She sat up and the heat of her fever caused her damp clothing to wick up in licks of pale steam.

Her hair dripped icy water down her spine.

O lord, she said, if you are not nothing, if you can hear my prayers, please allow your wretched servant to die where she lies here and now.

And she waited, her hands outspread, but there was no bolt of lightning. She did not die.

Around her mouth, the rash had grown tight and fiery; it had pushed out into larger pulsing bumps, into the true pox.

And then she said, O lord, even if you do not exist, or if you do exist and will not kill me now, then I who find myself most unhappily still alive, I who most unhappily do exist, must be the one to kill me now.

She considered. She was below the cliffs of the hillside, and returning up the steep slope was laughable, impossible. Even crawling, she could not find her way up to throw herself off. And, she thought, if she broke her neck without killing herself, her sufferings would rebound upon her a hundredfold.

She looked at the river before her, calm and shining and innocent now the cloud was gone, and thought of putting rocks in the sack, wading out too far to come up for breath. But she did not know where she could find the force to do any of this.

Instead, downstream, a large brown mass came out of the trees into the shallows.

It is a bear, the voice said to her.

A bear, she said aloud. It is indeed.

And behind the bear were two much smaller bears, mere babes, unweaned and round and tufted, that sat upon their rears and watched their mother.

She thought it wonderful that if the bear ate her, some part of her would enter the bear's body, would flow through her milk into the bodies of the babes, and the babes would grow to adult bears and would have their own babes, and some small part of who she had been would live somewhere within the blood and meat and fat of all of them.

The only kind of eternity there would be for her, for she would never have babes herself, and no one still alive would remember her after she was gone.

She stood and nearly fell but did not. With her stick, she pushed her poor body toward the bear. Every few steps she stopped to pant and ensure that the bear was still where she had last seen it.

I arrive, goodly bear, she said to it. Stay where you are.

She waked without having known she had lain down to sleep. On sharp gravel.

It had not been a long sleep, for the bear and her cubs remained.

She tried to stand but her feet could not walk now. Curious.

Crawl, girl, the voice said kindly now. On your hands and knees. Here you are.

The sack tied to her hips dragging behind, a tail like a beaver's.

The mother bear was fishing. She was slapping her paw on the water, slapping fish out of the river.

Every so often, the baby bears cried out in their high voices. They wrestled, grew bored, dipped their paws into the water. How like children they were. How like the child Bess.

The mother bear came out of the shallows to feed them, and they nuzzled her wide belly and nursed as she brought a fish to her mouth with her paws and ate it.

The girl crawled forth so slowly that the babes had finished their eating by the time she was close enough to see their faces.

After some time, she thought to see if she could stand, and she could, though wobbly and uncertain. She came closer to the bear and her cubs so slowly that it was as though she were sliding on her own grease like a snail.

The mother bear at last stopped in her movements and began to watch the girl nearing.

The black snout and skull and shoulders made a terrible arrowhead pointing at her.

All within the girl told her to run away, but she did not; the girl came nearer.

The babes made little moans of curiosity and sniffed the air in her direction.

They were potbellied, bright-eyed. They ran up to her, and with their snouts and their small paws, they touched her feet in the boots.

They were too young to know human savagery. They thought of her as a friend.

She could not speak words of the mouth, her mouth would not obey her, and so she spoke words of the heart, and the words said that she loved the baby bears; they reminded her of her best-beloved Bess.

Still, the mother bear did not come with her paws like maces, with her teeth, her devilish claws.

The girl forced herself closer until she put her body between the mother and her cubs.

She looked upon the mother bear, who looked upon her. Then, spilling the bright hot pain in her head, she bent and with her hand she touched the cubs.

Then the mother bear did stand upon her rear feet. In the shallow water she stood and she moved ungainly and she came back making huffing noises and clacking her deadly teeth. The girl squared her body to the bear. She dropped her stick. She opened her hands. She spread her arms.

She had believed herself to be brave enough to watch her longed-for end come toward her, but she was not.

She closed her eyes. She held her breath. She waited gratefully for the swipe and the knives of claws across her neck and the breath stopping where it would be cut from her.

And now in her face the mother bear's hot fish breath, wild sharp humphs.

Goodbye to all the wide world I have so loved, the girl said inside her head. Goodbye, my glassblower, my girl Bess, I am sorry there will be no eternity to see you in.

But there was no sharpness of claw or teeth upon her skin. The moment stretched until it broke.

When the girl opened her eyes, she saw that the mother bear had gone around her. She was on her four paws again and shepherding her cubs up the bank. Where the rock was steep, she took each babe gently by the scruff and lifted them up. Then, with the strange grace of her heavy limbs, the bear went on her way forward and was gone.

Too paltry a bit of flesh, the girl knew herself, then, too plainly diseased that even the bear could smell the disease upon her; she was not even worthy of killing.

She would not be delivered from the full force of her sufferings.

She let herself sink down upon the nearest boulder. She put her hands upon her face and wept.

And then she lay upon the ground, all the strength of her limbs gone.

The sack she untied and put behind her head as a pillow.

The hard metal in there, the hatchet and pewter cup and knife, bit at her head, but she did not care.

It was pleasant here, though cold. The river was shallow and wide. The water was a lovely slate color. The fishing birds fell as darts into the water then scooped their bodies up again joyously, falling and scooping, and the rain had gone and the afternoon sun poured down thick and pale and good over everyone.

Her fever roved through her, she let it, and the smallpox swallowed her body in dark bloom. This thing she had carried with her own bones and flesh and fought with would be far more deadly than any foe.

O, she thought, and inside her perhaps she was laughing darkly at the absurdity, all that wasted fear to find the foe too, too solidly within her own small self.

21.

No redemption, for there had proved no god to do the redeeming. A nought, an abscess, a great and teeming hole.

The men of her own country had always felt this nothing deep within them; they felt it twist and strain at the center of them, and they believed the sensation to be eternity. They grew up twisted inside around this nothing; it was like the scars after an early wound that deformed them around it, and so twisted, they became terrible and frightened and loud and hungry. It gave them a need to set their boots upon everything they saw.

She felt death rushing over the distances, flying near; it would soon be upon her, and she would die.

A little sleep, a little slumber, a little folding of the hands to rest.

The ghost of the glassblower settled upon the rocks beside her; she could almost feel him all along her side.

And into her mind came the moments every day before the child Bess awakened, the delicate tracery of her eyelashes on her cheeks and the small veins in blue tributaries across her eyelids as the sun grew stronger; and the child gave a sigh and opened her eyes, which sharpened out of dull sleep. Then there was pleasure reflected there at the sight of her own person. What a privilege it was to witness someone you loved awakening to the new day, to the joy of seeing your own face.

Only this girl idiot in her crystalline wisdom had known what all the wise and witty never would. There could be no fight in this world, only submission.

22.

Once she had had a door within her that she could lock against the bad thoughts.

In her sickness, the door had been broken open.

Let there be pain, and there was pain.

It rose up hideous, her anger at the minister dragging along his wife, his daughter, the girl, in his greed for riches. And neither the child Bess nor she was ever asked if they wished to come.

For what is a girl but a vessel made to hold the desires of men.

Though the minister, the new master, had been well loved by the household at first, in short weeks, he became disliked, then hated. He was always cold and needed the fire built up, expensively; he was always complaining of the sluttishness of the washing up and the laxness of the servants' bodies to attend to his, and he dared throw a fried smelt back into the face of the redoubtable cook for serving the food not crisp enough to his tongue. Then, after the dissolution of the household, he was deeply truly hated. In the kitchen, a song rose, containing all the many bad fates they wished would befall him in the savage country, an arrow through his temple, his pale hair scraped off, his body dropped dead off a cliff and let to suffer a broken neck as the carrion birds dug into his guts, a crocodile rushing up in its steam and fire from a river-bank to carry the minister off in its jaws, the men of the land roasting him alive as if he were a feasting pig and gobbling down his tender blond flesh. The girl, who was clever at such songs and hated the new master deep for robbing her of her mistress's love, had a large hand in the songmaking.

In swiftness, the house had been sold, the mistress's bad son Kit set up in his own household, valuables packed away for taking, necessary items purchased, the mistress's luscious wardrobe donated in an act of stunning generosity to the theater companies of her friends.

The slight and sparrowlike poet-player rubbing a gown's velvet voluptuousness against his cheek.

Then, together on shipboard, the four remaining souls of the household bade farewell to the filthy smoky city with its damp stone walls that contained within them so many hidden rooms of astonishing elegance.

The crossing was brutal and the child Bess, so simple and dumb, barely survived. Then setting her first footstep on the wild earth of this new country, the child Bess had felt the badness of the place and the english project in it, and from that moment forth, she refused to eat. She laid her body down and clenched her teeth and starved, yet she lasted through anguished months of winter when all around were dying in such numbers the frozen ground could not be dug quick enough to bury them.

The mistress had eaten what she by law was not allowed to own, the lead white paint she had once put on her skin to whiten it, the carmine to brighten her lips and cheeks, the blackberry stain for her white hairs, until she was turned sudden hag in the new world, having eaten up all her tricks of youth and beauty which had ensnared her second husband. And for some time, it was whispered by the most horror-quaked of the men that the mistress was revealed a witch, as the quickness of the transformation took their breath away, and all knew that witches were old, blear-eyed, pale, foul, and full of wrinkles. And the mistress being a witch would explain the curse of death and sorrow and hunger that had befallen the settlers in the fort. But the minister her husband stood as an angry god in the way of the whispers.

No one but the girl and the mistress knew how this sweet nothing of a child Bess, this pure baby inside her mind, could make herself die of horror in a way that far more intelligent men and women could not do, for their courage failed them.

The girl had been lying beside the child Bess as the last of her life ebbed sweetly away and felt in her skin the moment that the child Bess died.

For some time, she alone knew of the death, and she shook so that her teeth clacked in her head and was as aggrieved as a dumb beast of the fields.

She could not allow her child Bess to be taken, the girl thought. In this place, the bodies of the diseased dead were stacked ten deep to await the thaw of the earth for burial, and rats crawled freely among the corpses until, just as the pigs and chickens and cows and horses and dogs and cats and songbirds and insects had been eaten, even the vermin that crawled among the dead were eaten. And hurriedly the girl washed the body of her Bess, the neck, the cheeks, the ears, the white limbs, and dressed her in her best gown. Then she herself went out and with her ungloved hands ripped down from the miserable houses the wood that she burned on the ground enough to dig up some inches of thawed earth. Then she burned again, and many hours it took of burning and digging until she had dug a shallow grave for her girl.

In the blue twilight of that day, her last day among her people, the girl and the mistress and minister came out solemnly, and the minister gave a simple prayer for such a simple creature as their child Bess. Then they lowered her in her white linen shroud into the ground and all wept, for this small true beauty had left the world forevermore.

The girl watched the earth eat the child Bess and was shattered; she went inside to her bed that she had shared with her Bess and smelled the scent of her hair on the pillow and wished herself to die of a thought as well. But hers was too animal a vitality and she could not.

In the night, though, she woke to a strangeness in the air and saw the minister's and the mistress's cots empty. She crept outside to the hidden courtyard where they were standing in the dark, whispering, and there was also the governor there and his two minions and four soldiers guarding the doors. And they seemed to have made a decision, for they all went out together silently back to where they had so recently put the child Bess into the ground. And there the soldiers took shovels and dug the child Bess up, and it was simple, for the earth had not yet hardened. When the corpse was lifted out, they split the shroud and there the pale dear face was again, shining dim in the torchlight, hair gleaming golden. Soon the hair caught the icy blowing snow in it and whitened. Then a soldier stepped near to the girl's body and raised an ax above his head to split her skull open, and the girl, watching in horror, knew without being told that a body that did not die of disease in this place was a body that still bore good meat. And she could not move; she watched, frozen, as they began to butcher the child.

She only stirred from her terror when she saw the mistress, still sunk to her knees on the frozen ground, weeping in her grief, reaching her hands out eagerly for a morsel of the brain that they had fried in the pan upon the fire. And watching this woman, the only mother the girl had ever had in the world, weep and greedily reach, the girl rose from her hiding place and ran into the shameful circle and with all her force sent the mistress flying; she screamed and kicked and bit, but they shut her up by shoving her to the ground and putting a boot upon her head, and her mouth was full of frozen mud and she could not breathe.

She lay there thinking until the soldier shifted his weight and quick-quick she rolled out from under him and was gone; she flew into the house and in a trice even in the darkness gathered all the good faithful things she had marked as useful, putting on all her own and the child Bess's gowns and stockings, the boots she'd stolen off the gentleman's dead son, the mistress's thickest cloak, her warmest gloves, and put into the sturdiest sack the two coverlets, the pewter cup, the hatchet, the flint. She found the knife hidden among the minister's papers and slipped it into her pocket, then the vizard of hardened silk that the mistress bore on her face on the brightest days to keep her skin from further browning, a button between her teeth to hold it there, and beneath its erasure of her face, she grew strong.

Down the rows of the dying and the dead she ran with the hood up and the vizard blacking out her face, and should those who could have looked up, they would have seen the very angel of death flying through their rows.

Back out into the cold and moonless dark, to the hard icy snow, the place in the palisade through which someone only as slight as she could pass. The breath caught in the mask upon her face made her tingle with warmth.

But waiting for her in the shadows was the minister, his lips newly greased, and he stepped out and seized her by the throat and lifted her against the rough wood of the palisade, and there was no one near to stop him from murdering her. The button fell out of her teeth; the vizard fell off her face. Her hot skin was seared in the sudden cold. For a long time, she hung from his hand choking, and death did crawl in like spiders from the edges of her vision.

He hissed in her face, Know ye not that to whom ye yield yourselves servants to obey, his servants ye are to whom ye obey; whether of sin unto death or of obedience into righteousness?

She could not speak a word, her vision was nearly gone, but with this, she felt in her pocket with the last of her forces and took out the knife, which slid from its scabbard in her pocket, and thrust it into the minister's belly.

They both fell and lay upon the ground, the minister's hot blood and his viscera spilling out and he moaning loud, and she gasping her breath back again; then she regained her senses just as footsteps thudded in nearing. She put the knife back into her pocket and thrust first the sack and then her body through the tiny hole in the palisade. Then she heaved herself up out of the cursed stinking place and ran through the blackened corn away from her sin into the known terrors and greater unknown terrors of the wilds.

As she lay dying, she wept, too weak to stop the nightmare from returning, these moments she had shoved away and locked behind the door in her all this time of flight.

Her sin was the sin of murder, and this was a sin nearly as bad as denying god, which she also sinned at doing; but surely she was defending her life and the minister would have killed her gladly. In truth, it was more the horror of what they had done to the body of her sweet girl Bess that made her weep now in her last hours upon the earth.

She saw it again and again; the door could no longer close, and she could not push back the seeing.

23.

She heard a flapping, and with a swelling of hope, she thought of seraphim swimming invisibly through the element of the air.

When she made an effort to open one eye, however, she saw a vulture settling down beside her, his wings outstretched, fixing her with a humorous glint in his eye.

Yes, she thought, this is right. Old carrion bird, bringing your reek of death to me.

Her mind rose into the air as though it had taken flight, and it looked across the large green expanse of the world with the jagged thrusts of the mountains into the sky and the sweeps of forests and the veins of rivers and the constant gnashing teeth of the ocean's white waves.

And in the air, now, she had a single bright flare, a vision that extended her life vastly beyond this moment of her dying, both in the greater sweep and in the smaller grains.

24.

Within the vision, she saw a second self, an imagined self, opening her eyes.

The day had grown older. The vulture had stepped closer.

The vision self pushed herself to sitting. The river dipped and dazzled in her eyes. She dragged her body painfully, over hours, up the stones to the edge of the forest. The mother bear, in leaving, had discarded a fish upon the bank, and it was still fresh, shaded by a tender new fern. She fell upon it. She ate it in small bites, raw, and tasted nothing. Each bite exhausted her. She chewed even the bones.

The vulture despaired of her and flew away.

She ate until she fell asleep cradling the remains of the fish and woke to late afternoon. Up over the edge of the forest she dragged herself, into the twilight of shadows there. She found blowdown trees fallen in a

V shape, mossed over thickly, and wedged her body inside. In the warmth of rotting trees, she slept.

For days she lay there, crawling to the woods to shit, to drink water. The pox raged over her in fever. She was still too weak to coax a fire to life, but the sun shone and warmed the world, and she had luck in the weather, for there was no rain to chill her and the nights were mild and the coverlets kept the chill at bay.

Her body drew itself out of its illness slowly, but her diseases were pressed deep into the skin. Her face felt like granite, rough and hard, to her fingers.

In those days of fever and illness, her dreams were terrors innumerable and she often woke screaming.

In her moments of clarity, she found the place where fallen stones in the river had made a natural weir, where fish were held when she chased them, and all she needed to do was stand dizzied with weakness and walk with her skirts outspread above the water to trap the fish, then bend and catch the fish with her hands. She ate fish beyond satiety. She ate without pleasure, only to fatten herself.

After a week of this, she was strong enough to search out better shelter. She moved up the river, sometimes crawling. Not far, less than an hour's movement later, she found a spit of land that rose in sharp embankment over the river, near to water and fish but protected on three sides. Here she sat on the sunwarmed stones and felt if not good then not nearly dead.

She was weak; she was deeply ill. But the place itself told that here she could live.

Her luck held in a span of dry warm days. She fished in the mornings and gathered the bright new berries in the woods and set most on the flat stones to dry in the sun as she rested in the shade in the afternoons. At twilight each day, she worked on her hovel, fitting together stones she had selected carefully, mortaring them with dark clay she dug with her hatchet from a streambed and carried back in her sack. The house she was making was small, twice the length of her body in both directions, with a single opening facing the river. She could make the roof so low that she would only just be able to stand in it.

And she saw how in two cycles of the moon this other self was strong enough that, with rests, she could climb to the top of her house and tie split branches into a tight roof. She covered this first roof thickly with grassy sod that in the rains of late summer grew together into a luscious green mound, then began growing down the stone walls of her house. She kept a hole open above for the smoke of her fire to leave. She wove a door out of skinned willow sticks and thought it insufficient for wolves and large cats and bears, and lashed it with grapevines to two more thicknesses of doors made of skinned willow sticks until she had a thick barrier through which even the sharpest wind did not blow.

She found a kind of cane that, when juiced upon a rock and wetted and massaged, did make a soapy foam; and with this, she washed the filth off her body and the rags of her clothing, and beat the dirt from them with stones, and set them upon the hot rocks to dry. And naked she went into the water of the river and held her breath and knelt and scrubbed the filth and many insects from her body. Then, still naked, she went into her hovel and scrubbed the stone floor over and over with the soapy foam until she felt that all of the vermin that had hidden in the cracks were gone.

She built shelving of stones and sticks, and made fast her supplies of dried berries, dried fish, dried mushrooms, nuts, and covered it all with a tight-woven screen to keep the fieldmice from entering and eating it all. She played with traps and snares until she began to catch the small beasts, then the muskrat and otter and squirrel. She used their skins to make a hat and mittens and slippers, and turned them softside, furside, in.

And thus the wounds and broken bones of her body healed, and she filled her days with industry.

Then she saw how, deep in autumn, as the sky darkened ominous with coming winter, she glimpsed herself in a still cold pool and saw herself wizened, ancient, hair gone white at the root with her past diseases. Many of her teeth were gone. A mad charwoman of sixty years of age, she looked, and she laughed at herself because there was no one to impress.

In the winter, the fire in the hovel was her best companion, for the ghost of the glassblower was gone for good now. She spoke to it over the long dark nights, the gray days. She drew the stories out that she told aloud so long that they took many days and nights to finish. The fire cracked and spat and coughed, it groaned, it sighed with the snow that came in through the hole of her roof and sizzled upon the heat. The moisture from her breath loosed mud from above, and it dropped down upon her in sudden shocking clods out of the dark.

Sometimes the voice returned to her and she spoke to it in disputations.

And in the vision, spring came again and she emerged into the cold light, feeling as though she had woken from the longest night terror yet. Her madness had passed through her and left a kernel of herself behind. She was still weak, she would never be strong again, but she knew she could do anything if she only moved carefully enough. She worked with patience and most days spent a long time resting upon a warm rock, thinking.

Sometimes she stopped in her labors and saw with a thrill how beautiful the world was, how exquisite the purple mountains sometimes rising, a trick of optics, at the edge of sight, how joyous the blue birds chasing each other like scraps of windblown sky.

A pureness of happiness coursed through her and left her ravished.

She watched as, in her long and solitary rhythms, this other self lived alone in the wilderness and time was forgotten.

One winter she had barely enough to eat. Another winter a stag died sudden in the meadow over the hill, and she could drag back meat enough for a whole season and make a crude dress of hide for herself.

During the long dark nights of her solitude, she thought often of the half man, half beast who had stoned her, finally arriving at a guess near the truth of his life, how he may have been an early spanish or english man who escaped, who lived beyond the boundaries of the powhatan, how, certainly, they knew of him, how possibly they protected him from a distance, for she could not imagine that they would stand a man of the others upon their land unless they felt some form of duty to him.

For she knew that they knew of her in her stone hovel; she saw the footprints in the mud in the lands near her sometimes or the human form moving at the edges of her sight.

Once, she looked up at the riverbank to see a woman of their people on the other side, gazing at her. And she gazed back, and with a flare of the light of friendship in her, she raised her hand. But the other turned and vanished and was seen no more.

She knew with certainty then that if she was living there she was living only with their tolerance; and if they had not come to speak to her, they had no willingness to show her friendship.

And often she thought in terror of what would happen if they would lose their tolerance of her and want to rid themselves of her gnatlike irritation there on their lands, if she would wake in the night to human bodies within her little hovel.

Then I would die at least looking upon another human face, she said aloud, and laughed darkly, for this was the extent of her ache, that she would welcome this, for at least she would know a human again.

And she knew she must be contented by living alone; for though she was sick unto her soul for want of love and human conversation, she was still a stranger here; she had imposed herself upon this place, and their acceptance of the fact of her was a gift of grace enough.

She felt very ancient and very sick in her final year alone in the wilderness. She had lost count at twenty-five or twenty-six years of age. She could have been no younger than thirty-two and no older than forty.

After so long in her solitude, she saw the trees and the clouds and the distant mountains begin to grow human faces within their depths; the

cold water of her stream was full of silvery faces that laughed and gri-
maced up at her. And she did not always feel the cold winds of solitude
in her.

She watched the final springtime of this, her long extended beauteous
vision of a life beyond her actual moment of death; she watched the vast
swarms of pale birds with pink necks as they landed and stripped the
trees of their leaves and fruit, and plastered the ground with their white
scat. She watched them fly off in vast and noisome clouds. She understood this new phenomenon of overabundance to be born of the arrival
of yet more of her people in the land. There was a new imbalance, a
strangeness unsustainable. Henceforth, there would be far too much in
some directions and in others a wretched poverty. Already the purple
birds that had sung so sweet and been so common when she arrived had
almost entirely gone, after their transit in the autumn.

She had a chair that she had made with her own hands one winter, whittled from good strong oak with her knife, the seat woven from strips of
softened cane, and it was deep and comfortable, as good as any of the
english governor's from the settlement a lifetime ago. She dragged her
chair out to the sun and there sat watching the play of light upon the
shadows and the movement of clouds, and she let the voices come to
speak to her full.

The mistress's commands and jokes, the child Bess's babble, the
quips of the suitors and players and poets, the senseless sounds of the
glassblower's language soft in her ear.

Now it was in her vision of an alternative ending that the oldest and the strangest of the voices returned to her although she was sure that it was an echo of a long-dead conversation.

The end is nigh, the voice said. Do you rue the course your life reborn hath taken?

No, she said, considering. For I am a woman of good fortune.

And do you rue the loss in the wilderness of your god?

In truth, I know not numbers, but I do know that nought from nought remains nought.

Are you sorry to leave this place that has allowed you these years of life?

No, she said, for the blight of the english will come to this remoteness as well. It will spread into this land and infect this land and devour the people who were here first; it will slaughter them, diminish them. The hunger inside the god of my people can only be sated by domination. They will dominate until there is nothing left, then they will eat themselves. I am not of them. I will not be.

And is there nothing that you could have done to change the final shape of your story?

I who was born nothing and am nothing? With this small body and this small life?

You could have made your way to the others, the people of the land, who have taken in some men and women and children of the fort and kept them alive.

And she thought of this, of the long life she might have had among the other people with their customs and their gods and their foods and their language, and she felt a grief and an anger at herself for her fear of others that outweighed her fear of the wilds.

———

And even within her vision, during her long dying of smallpox and fever and exhaustion and hunger on the riverbank, with the vulture spreading its wings in anticipation near her curled form, she thought of the men who had followed her at the waterfall not days earlier; she thought that perhaps they had not meant evil, that perhaps they had seen her illness and madness, and had meant to help her.

She saw how, if they had carried her back to their village, everyone who would have touched her would have been marked invisibly with illness; a radiant tracery of illness would have passed from hand to hand, and it would have been she through this touch who would have brought death with her into the village. And the death would have spread between family near and travelers far, mothers would have died, babes died, entire families dying together on the ground; she would have been an unwitting extension of the settlement so arrogant so dirty upon the river James, of those men who call themselves of god who tore up the trees and burned them, and took the fish the clean air the land the game. Her body complicit though her mind would not have wanted death to seed itself among them through her touch. And though she grieved for her death that neared, she was also glad that her own illness had not been the spark that had touched the others and set whole villages ablaze.

Yet even in the vision, she found herself yearning for another soul to have spent her life with. Against the resistance of other minds, one's thoughts are pulled out of their comfortable shapes, and true thinking begins. And to have another body to minister to her body's needs and take in turn her loving ministrations. A hand to hold, a face to love. Humans were never meant to live alone.

Then all sped up in the last part of this second self's life, and the final winter came like the shadow of a cloud drawn forever over the face of the sun. The cold rushed down from the mountain.

And in a dream, she was a hoary beast making a slow advancement over the land, each pebble outlined and beloved by her eye, and on the wind, she smelled everything that had happened in each place. What might have been sere and sterile was not, she knew now; death touched every place that had been touched by man; in each fistful of death, there were hundreds of deaths writ small through time, some animal bleeding the blood of its heart into the earth, the death of a sapling rotted and chewed into soil, the death of a worm or a beetle or a grub, all death living in the brown of the earth, which was the brown of what had once been living. Everywhere she looked was thick with death; all the earth held the ghost of what had passed before.

She saw deeper. She saw the ghosts of everything that had come before and had once also lived in the rays of the sun. She saw the silent and invisible force that animated all creation.

She had once believed that in the deepest reaches of everything was a nothing where men had planted god; but now she knew that deeper within that nothing was something else, something made of light and heat.

It was this light and heat that endured, that was everlasting. At the center was not nothing, no. Out of the light and the heat all goodness poured.

And then, in the vision, she found herself standing on ice and snow thick in the black night air, and she did not know where she was. She turned on her wobbly legs and saw a glow of fire coming through the chinks of her house. In her frozen hands, there was the hatchet; at her feet, a hole matte with water. She had been cutting a hole in the ice to fish in though it was deep into the night and the wind blew extreme cold.

Carefully, she shuffled away from the hole toward the gleam of her hovel in the black. But her head was light, the ice slippery, and her foot slid, and she felt herself falling and had enough time to know as her body fell through the snow-thick air that her bones were too fragile and would not bear the landing. When the ice kissed hard on her cheekbone, she was stunned. Worse than falling was the sickening crack from her hip, and the strange weight in her side. She moved her hands down her body until she felt the wooden hilt of the hatchet, its head buried beneath her ribs. Her old friend had bitten her. Heat was escaping her body in great wet gouts. Her hands were black with it.

She held the hatchet where it was inside her body with one hand, and on the heel of the other and on her one good knee, she began to crawl over the ice toward her house. She stopped every few feet to breathe. Her breath rasped against the air. Her hand and knee went numb. Everything belonging to her was a blunt instrument, and the only thought in her head was forward. She left a slick black on the ice behind her.

She crawled up the bank to the cabin and pulled herself inside. The door shut behind her and the fire had nearly burnt itself out. The cabin was cold, and with the last of her strength, she pushed a log into the embers and sat until her dizziness faded. Her tunic was stiff with blood, and the noise of her breathing filled the cabin and made it small.

She knew she would do her body grievous harm by pulling the hatchet out, but it had become unbearable to her mind. Upon her un-broken hip she lay, then she seized the hatchet with her hand, and in a swift movement, she pulled it from her while in the same moment with the other hand she pressed fresh fur to her side. Night fell in her eyes. When she opened them again, daylight was coming through the smoke hole, and she was lying in her own cold blood.

She was old and full of days, she told herself in this vision of a distant death. She pulled her body toward her sleeping hide and climbed under it and put her head beneath its darkness to feel darkness come into her.

She slept, and in her sleep, she smiled because she saw glories of sundazzle and water and the night sky white with stars; she was flying once more effortless across the land.

The loss of a star dims not the splendor of the constellations; she did not have the force to remember which of her voices had said this.

And she fell out of this alternative vision of a longer false life.

To be alone and surviving is not the same as being alive, she understood.

And if she could in fact rouse herself to healing, if she could chase away the vulture of death, she would not choose this life that was shown to her, though the beauties of the world were without limit and the grace given to encounter more of them would have been an astonishing gift. Though there was satisfaction in the work of her body and her hands, though mere survival was a triumph, she understood now that the long loneliness of such a life she would never choose for herself.

25.

The girl's ragged breathing grew shallow.

And then time, each a lengthening span of it, passed between the breaths.

Soon the vulture would hop close, then closer; it would bow its stinking head in benediction.

Then other vultures would coast down, descend upon her form with a riot of wings, would fall upon the girl's skin and flesh. And up out of the earth into her body would rise the worms. Her body become feast.

In days her skull would be carried away by a coyote. What had been her rib cage, her spine, would be dragged into the mossy edge of the forest and left in place. There, between the ribs, an oak sapling would press up its head, and this small green life would push quick up in a blaze of spring and summer sunlight, within months hardening into sapling. By winter, the trunk would weave through her bones, at the height the girl herself upright had once been, and by spring again, what of her bones would not have been dragged off by the little animals would have grown into the roots of the tree that would one day be a vast old emperor of the forest, and the trunk would grow up around the bone, and the last of her would stay for centuries within its living wood, a memory.

In the last moments, a peace stole over her. Her vision of her second self had taught her how to die.

For, inches beyond this face of hers and in the profoundest sufferings of her body, the world went on in its grand and renewing and wholly indifferent beauty.

And the earth itself uncovered its shining face and to her now revealed itself in a litany of wonder:

The spring unleashing its winter-coiled power, the joy of living.

And the tender green of the new grass, the green of bursting vibrancy.

And the gold of the old grass of the last year, the gold of sustenance.

And the stones, with their lives so slow that to all impatient moving creatures of animated life they did appear unmoving, but even the stones she understood now did meet and mate, did erupt and splinter, did rub to powder stone upon stone and stone upon water and stone upon air, so that in the long scale of their lives the stones saw within themselves incredible vitality.

And the restless spinning of the water down the river, each drop promiscuous in its combining and recombining, water a brazen laughing ecstatic element, rising in its own breathing of itself into the air or running headlong with its countless fellow drops down toward the sea.

And the good warmth flowing down through the element of the heavens and casting its warming rays upon the earth where, melting the frost and heating the loam, it waked the worms to frenzy in their various darkness, and they drew with the motion of their bodies their long embroideries of empty tunnels in the many feet beneath where she lay, bringing veins of living air deep into the blackness between the surface so that all the loam was crazed with the tiny tunnels of the worms.

And the sky in its similar eternal churning blues and pales, and the lonely heap of cloud in the west, frothing and delicate and whipped and with silvery creases deepening to violet, shifting in subtle formations in its sail to the east, and even as it came larger in nearing, she felt the urge to prick it so that it would stay where it was, so perfect, the way a child with the cruelty in his heart soothed by science fastens a green moth into gorgeous stillness with his pins and boards; or a limner fixes a moment of beauty forever with his oils and canvas and the art of his sensibility; or a hunter who with dark magic stuffs the beasts he has slain with horsehair and cotton, and thus turns ferocity of nature into a tamed and sempiternal statue of glower and fang.

And those two swifts engaged overhead in their courtship and mating, never ceasing in their flight, darting and thrashing upward into the highest coldest air until they rose to the very boundaries of her sight and became but specks in the highest blue; until together they came and ceased their winging and spiraled downward in the satisfaction of their lust; until, nearly dashing their bodies upon the rocks beneath, they spread their wings and flapped and came apart and rose together into the sky again to renew their intoxication with the other's body; how she envied them the sap rising within, the white hot final burst of their small bodies' fullest joy, the pleasure that makes for life. For the glory of the world was the glory of such freeness, such gladness, she understood.

Sun with earth and water with water and beast with beast.

The only thing meant to be alone is the good sun that shines its endlessly giving heat and light, that one great creator who alone can burn against the nothingness.

On her tongue now: the taste of an orange.

An ant was crawling on her forehead, and she did not have the force to remove it. She tracked its many tiny feet across the stretch of her skin and, through tracking, felt herself within the ant, all her own jagged pores of skin beneath, the delicacies of her flesh, the salt and sweetness of her blood.

Rejoice, small ant, she thought, in your one life, though too soon dimmed it shall be.

This would be the last thought she would have.

And the final moment of the girl's life was like the end of all lives, whether large and renowned or small and unknown and forgotten.

The pause between breaths lengthened until there was no more breath to put an end to the pause. The organs shut down, the guts, the lungs, the heart. Last to end was the brain, in a flare all went jagged within, and there was lightning in colors wondrous beyond vision.

Then everything that made the girl herself through the shedding of time did come out of her, and this essential self of her passed into the air, and the wind that blew over her prone body lifted it into the larger, higher world. She had been born a babe out of the darkness out of nothing; she had sparked to first breath and first wonder. As is the truth of all the people who have walked and will walk upon the earth, she returned at last to all she had been before life.

For there was nothing there, no angels, no harps, no gates, no fires singeing the sins back into the sinner, no hungry spirits wandering the land and standing in the cold outside the firelight of the living. There was only wind drawing itself endlessly over the dark crowns of the pines, over the face of the water, over the mountains' icy peaks, over the great wide golden stretches of the teeming land. The wind passed, even as it is passing now, over all the people who find themselves so dulled by the concerns of their own bodies and their own hungers that they cannot stop for a moment to feel its goodness as it brushes against them. And feel it now, so soft, so eternal, this wind against your good and living skin.

Acknowledgments

I owe my deep gratitude to many people who made this book possible:

Everyone at the Radcliffe Institute for Advanced Study, the Guggenheim Foundation, the Civitella Ranieri Foundation, and the American Academy in Berlin;

My readers: Laura van den Berg, Elliott Holt, Stephanie DeGooyer, Megan Mayhew Bergman, Hernan Diaz, Jami Attenberg, Dr. Joyce Chaplin, Alison Fairbrother, Patricia Liu, my sensitivity readers, and my German translator, Stefanie Jacobs, for her eleventh-hour save;

My agents, Bill Clegg and Marion Duvert, and the other marvelous people at the Clegg Agency: Simon Toop, MC Conners, Nikolaus Slackman, Rebecca Pittel, Kirsten Wolf, Laura Southern; as well as Kassie Evashevski at Anonymous Content;

My Riverhead family: Sarah McGrath, Jynne Dilling Martin, Claire McGinnis, Geoff Kloske, Helen Yentus, Delia Taylor, Grace Han, Lauren Peters-Collaer, Ashley Sutton, Melissa Solis, Caitlin Noonan,

ACKNOWLEDGMENTS

David Hough, Christina Caruccio, Nicole Wayland, Claire Vaccaro, Denise Boyd, Stephanie Hwang, Kitanna Hiromasa, and the late Lucia Bernard;

My Hutchinson Heinemann family, especially Ailah Ahmed, Laura Brooke, and Linda Mohamed;

My family: Clay, Beckett, and Heath.

This book is for my sister, Sarah True, who has spent decades pushing her body to the limits of human ability, and who, in the process, has made her soul radiant.